# Sonrise Stable
# Clothed With Thunder

Vicki Watson

Illustrated by Becky Raber

Printed in the United States by Morris Publishing®
3212 East Highway 30
Kearney, NE  68847
1-800-650-7888

*Hast thou given the horse strength? hast thou clothed his neck with thunder? Canst thou make him afraid as a grasshopper? the glory of his nostrils is terrible. He paweth in the valley, and rejoiceth in his strength...*

Job 39:19-22

# Sonrise Stable Characters *(Horses in Parentheses)*

Grandma
*(Kezzie, Sassy)*

| Lisa and Robert | Kristy and Eric | Julie *(Elektra)* and Jonathan |
| --- | --- | --- |
| Lauren | Rosie *(Scamper)* | Jared *(Scout)* |
| | Carrie *(Zach)* | Jessie *(Patches)* |
| | | Jamie *(Pearl)* |

Cats: June Bug, Katy, Jemimah

Dog: Tick

\* Always wear a helmet when you ride. Helmets are not depicted in the illustrations for artistic purposes only.

# Chapter 1

# Eohippus to Equus?

"Eohippus was the first horse. He lived sixty million years ago." Emily smiled and pointed to a small creature on her poster. Rosie looked at Carrie and frowned. She had seen illustrations of this creature many times in horse books, but she couldn't believe Emily was actually doing a demonstration on it.

"Eohippus was about twenty inches tall, with four toes on his front legs and three on the back. He lived in a marshy forest and ate leaves."

The 4-H club members listened attentively as Emily explained how, over millions of years, Eohippus evolved into the three-toed Mesohippus and Merychippus, then the single-toed Pliohippus, and finally the modern-day horse.

Rosie fidgeted. *That's not true! Why is she saying that?* She was halfway to her feet, about to declare that horses were created by God, when Carrie grabbed her arm and pulled her back into her seat. She nodded toward the back of the room, where the parents were seated. Rosie turned and caught her mother's eye.

Kristy signed to her, "Keep still. I have an idea."

When Emily finished her demonstration, everyone applauded politely. The next member went to the front of the room and began to explain the genetics of horse coat colors. Normally Rosie would have found the topic interesting, but she could not get her mind off the string of "-hippuses" that had magically turned into horses.

"What did Mom say?" Carrie whispered. Rosie's parents, Kristy and Eric, had recently adopted Carrie. The girls had been sisters for less than a week, but best friends for several years. Having been an only child for so long, Rosie was excited to have a sister. Their mother was a sign language interpreter, so Rosie was fluent in American Sign Language. Carrie was just beginning to learn it.

"She has some kind of plan," Rosie whispered back. "Not sure what that's supposed to mean."

After several more demonstrations, the meeting came to an end. While the other members hurried to the refreshment table, Rosie and Carrie headed straight for Kristy. "Mom, why didn't you let me say something? Now all the kids are going to believe what Emily said."

"And how were you going to convince them that horses didn't evolve?" Kristy asked.

Rosie turned to Carrie who gave her a sympathetic look, but didn't offer any suggestions. "Well, you know—God created the animals on the sixth day. That's what it says in the Bible, right?"

Kristy nodded. "Yes, and that's enough to settle it for me, but you probably need something more than that to convince these kids."

"But," Rosie sputtered. "What can I do now? Her demonstration is over."

"Why don't you and Carrie give one at the next meeting presenting the other side of the story?" Kristy suggested.

Rosie brightened. "Yeah! That's a great idea."

Carrie raised her eyebrows and clutched at her necklace. She ran her fingers over the heart-shaped locket her grandmother had given her when she was adopted.

"Aw, don't worry, Carrie. If we do it together it won't be so bad." *Won't be so bad* was an understatement. Rosie loved to talk. She was growing more excited by the minute about getting up in front of the group and explaining how God created everything in just six days, but she knew that her sister had been dreading having to give a demonstration.

"You'll have a few weeks to prepare. Let me make sure it's all right." Kristy started toward one of the advisors, while Rosie and Carrie joined the other kids for refreshments.

Rosie ran into the living room as soon as they got back to Sonrise Stable. "Grandma! Guess what?"

Grandma pushed a button to raise her recliner. "What's got you so wound up? I don't remember 4-H meetings ever being that exciting." She adjusted the position of her right leg, which was in a cast. She and her horse, Kezzie, had both been injured in an accident on a recent trail ride. Kristy and the girls were staying at her home to help with the housework and barn chores. Rosie and Carrie moved to each side of Grandma's chair.

"Emily gave her demonstration tonight on the evolution of the horse," Rosie began.

"Oh?"

"I wanted to say something in the middle of it, but Mom wouldn't let me."

"That would have been a little rude," Grandma said, "but I can imagine how you must have felt."

"Rosie and I are going to do a demonstration on the creation of the horse at the next meeting," Carrie added.

Grandma's eyes lit up. "I like it!"

"Can you help us look up facts on the internet to prove that all that stuff she said about Plimochippus and the rest of them isn't true?"

Kristy laughed. "That's partly why I didn't want you to say anything tonight, Rosie. There's no such animal as Plimochippus."

"I know, Mom! That's what I mean. I just have to convince the other kids."

"No. Slow down and think. I love your enthusiasm, but you need facts to back up your position. Emily didn't say Plimochippus. There never was any such animal. If you say things like that, no one will take you seriously."

"Oh." Rosie slumped down on the arm of the chair and rested her chin on her hand. Maybe this wasn't going to be as easy as she had thought.

Grandma carefully moved her bandaged arm away from Rosie. "Why don't we begin by researching what evolutionists claim about the evolution of the horse?"

"Okay, where's your laptop?" Rosie jumped off the arm of the chair and looked around the room.

"It's getting too late now," Kristy said. "You can start tomorrow when we get back from looking at the farm."

"Wow!" Rosie slapped her forehead. "I can't believe I forgot all about our farm." The girls' aunt, Julie, had heard that a horse farm, not far from her place, was going up for auction. She was convinced that the three families should join together and buy it. Julie would use part of the barn for her children's horses and the horses she was training, and Rosie's family would live at the farm with Grandma.

"Don't get your hopes up too high," Grandma warned. "It's not even close to being our farm yet. Even if we decide we want to buy it, other people will be bidding on it too."

Rosie nodded, then turned to Carrie and whispered, "I'm still going to call it our farm."

"I'm not sure you're ready for this, Mom," Kristy worried aloud.

"Aunt Lisa said it would be okay if Grandma rode around the farm on a four-wheeler," Rosie reminded her mother.

"Well, Nurse Lisa should have stayed here a while longer to keep an eye on her." Kristy sighed. "At least Eric will be with us this time if anything happens."

# Chapter 2

# Farm for Sale

Kezzie nickered when she saw Carrie approaching. "Good morning, girl! How are you feeling today?" Grandma's chestnut mare stuck her head over the stall door, and Carrie patted her neck. "You want out, don't you? Sorry, the vet says you need to rest for a few weeks."

"Poor Kezzie," Rosie said. "She and Grandma both hate being cooped up with nothing to do. At least now Grandma can help us with the demonstration."

Carrie walked over to the next stall. "And Kezzie has a new friend to keep her company."

A mule's head appeared over the front of the stall and turned to sniff at Kezzie. The mare pinned her ears and bit Sassy on the bridge of her nose. The mule squealed and jerked her head back.

"Sassy, I don't think she wants to be your friend." Rosie patted the mule's neck. "You better stay back."

The day after the trail riding accident, someone had given the girls' father the large, dark brown mule. Eric thought Sassy might make a good trail mount for Grandma since it had looked as if Kezzie's injury might prevent her from being ridden again. After several years of neglect, Sassy had become quite spoiled. Julie agreed to take the mule to her farm to train her. In the meantime she had ordered the girls to stay out of Sassy's stall.

"Kezzie's sure cranky after being in the stall all week," Carrie said.

"She wouldn't be so bad if old Mule Head would stop annoying her."

"Aw, I feel sorry for her. None of the horses like her." Carrie rubbed the mule's huge ears. Sassy let out a big sigh, and her eyelids drooped. "She loves this. I think she'd let me rub her ears all day."

"We don't have all day," Rosie said. "Bring Kezzie out. I'll get the hose."

"Sorry, big girl. I gotta go." Carrie picked up Kezzie's lead rope and led the mare out of her stall. Kezzie limped slightly, still favoring her right, front leg. Carrie positioned the horse on the concrete wash rack at the side of the barn.

Rosie turned the water on and aimed the stream from the hose at the injured leg. The vet had instructed the girls to hose Kezzie's leg twice a day to keep the swelling down.

Rosie flicked her wrist up and down so the water ran over Kezzie's leg. "I can't wait until we get the farm. It will be like Cousins Camp every day, only better since we'll have the indoor arena and a lot more land." She stepped back so she could run water over the other side of Kezzie's leg.

Carrie nodded. "Yeah, all the cousins except for Lauren. I wish they would move back here, so she could get a horse and join us. I like writing to her, but it would be even better if she lived nearby."

8

"Maybe she can spend next summer with us at the new farm," Rosie suggested.

"If we get it," Carrie said.

"Don't say 'if.'" Rosie raised the hose threatening to spray Carrie with it. "Of course we're getting it." She bent down and felt Kezzie's leg. "Has it been long enough yet?"

Carrie looked at her watch. "Five more minutes."

When they finished, Carrie led Kezzie back toward her stall. The horse stopped at the front of the barn, raised her head and whinnied to Scamper and Zach in the pasture. They looked up at her, then returned to grazing. "Come on, girl. It won't be too much longer before you can join them." Carrie tugged on the lead, and Kezzie reluctantly followed her into the barn.

Rosie ran to check on Scamper and Zach, while Carrie tossed Sassy and Kezzie a few flakes of hay. When they finished, the girls raced back to the house. Their dad had just pulled into the driveway.

Rosie stared at a large blue machine in the bed of the truck, then climbed onto the back bumper to get a better look. "Cool four-wheeler Dad!"

"A guy at work loaned it to me for Grandma to ride when we get to the farm. Don't get any ideas. We're not keeping it."

"That's okay. I'd rather ride Scamper anyway." Rosie hopped down. "Come on, Carrie. Let's see if Mom and Grandma are ready."

Tick, Grandma's Rottweiler puppy, was lying beside her in the living room. She jumped up when the girls ran in. Grandma got to her feet and adjusted the crutches under her arms. "I don't remember when I've been inside for so long. I can't wait to get out of this house!"

Rosie patted her leg. "Come on, Tick. You can go with us." The puppy wiggled in delight and ran after the girls. Rosie and Carrie climbed into the back seat of the truck, and Kristy lifted Tick in after them.

Carrie patted the dog's head. "What do you think, girl? Do you want to move to a new farm?" Tick barked and jumped onto her lap, pressing her nose against the window. "Oof! You're a little big to be a lapdog." Carrie slid over toward Rosie and pushed the puppy into the space between her and the window.

Kristy nudged Rosie. "Scoot over, kid. I need to get in here too."

Eric helped Grandma into the front and set her crutches in the truck bed.

"Here are the directions." Kristy offered Eric a crumpled piece of paper she had pulled out of her jeans pocket.

He waved the paper away. "I know where the farm is. You just go past Julie's and make a right at the stop sign. From there it's another mile, on the left side."

"I can't believe we're going to buy a farm—with an indoor arena," Rosie said.

10

"I guess this means I don't have to wait until you two get rich selling your book to finally get my riding arena," Grandma laughed.

Rosie looked over at Carrie. "We're still going to write it. Aren't we?"

"Yep." Carrie nodded and both girls smiled.

An hour later they turned onto Julie's road. Eric looked back at Kristy. "Should I stop at Julie's?"

"No, keep going. They're meeting us at the farm."

As they passed Julie's house, the road surface suddenly changed from pavement to gravel. Rosie could hear rocks thrown up from the tires pinging against the bottom of the truck. Eric tapped the brakes and slowed down. They traveled along a large cornfield, then stopped at a stop sign. "Seldom Seen Road. Yeah, I bet not too many people come out this far." Eric turned to the right and continued down the narrow country road.

On the right, flat farm fields stretched as far as the eye could see, with no houses in sight other than Julie's off in the distance. On the left, there were woods a ways back from the road. Rosie could see two huge trees up ahead on either side of what looked like the entrance to the farm. "There it is!" she shouted.

Kristy clapped her hands over her ears. "Not so loud. I'm sitting right beside you."

Rosie looked eagerly at the approaching property. The driveway was so overgrown with weeds you could barely tell it was there. A lonely post peeking out above the tall weeds looked as if it had at one time held a mailbox.

"I guess this is it." Eric started down the long drive, the truck bumping from one pothole to another. As they reached the end, the drive formed a circle with the house on the left and the barn on the right. Eric stopped the truck halfway between them. Carrie leaned over the dog and popped the door open. Tick leaped down, and the girls followed. Without even a glance at the house, they sprinted toward the stable.

Kristy looked at the house, and her mouth dropped open. "Oh, my word!" She opened her door but remained seated.

Grandma looked from the house to the barn and back to the house again.

Julie hurried over with her husband, Jonathan. "Well, what do you think?"

"I think you're out of your mind," Eric said. "Really, you're kidding about buying this, aren't you?"

They all turned to look at the large, old farmhouse. A bird flew out of a gaping hole in the roof. The glass in several second-story windows was shattered, and the front porch sagged dangerously in the middle.

Eric took off his hat and scratched his head. "I thought you said it needed a *little* work. This looks like it might be easier to tear it down and build a new house."

Grandma frowned. "It is a little rough looking."

For a moment Julie seemed unsure of herself, but she quickly recovered. She waved her hand. "Don't worry about the house. Come on and take a look at the barn."

Eric and Kristy stepped out of the truck, pushing through the tall weeds. Jonathan helped Eric unload the four-wheeler, and Grandma climbed aboard.

She looked over the controls. "How do I make this thing go and whoa?"

Eric started it and showed her how everything worked.

Grandma gunned the motor and took off with a lurch. She drove across the yard toward the stable.

Its white metal siding gleamed in the bright sunlight. Across the front of the barn were three sliding doors—a large one in the center and two smaller ones on each side. The door on the right was open, revealing two rows of stalls on either side of a wide aisle. Grandma drove the four-wheeler inside and stopped. "Why! This looks brand new."

"It is, practically," Julie said. "The owner had planned to open a boarding stable, but went bankrupt before he could finish. The barn is done, but they never got started remodeling the house."

The girls and Julie's kids ran up. "Come on, Grandma. You gotta see this!" Rosie said. They waved for the adults to follow them and took off for the riding arena that separated the two wings of the stable.

Grandma turned left past a large concrete wash area. Julie opened a gate and Grandma drove through. She stopped in the middle of the arena and shut the engine off.

"What do you think, Mom?" Julie asked.

Grandma looked from one end of the arena to the other and smiled. "Amazing! It's so big. I see why you were excited about this place."

One of Julie's twins, Jessie, tugged on Grandma's sleeve. "You won't believe this! Follow me." She led the group through another gate on the opposite side of the arena into the left wing of the stable. They went down the aisle which divided two more rows of stalls and stopped in front of a door at the back of the barn.

Grandma leaned forward. "I can't see in there. What is it?"

She started to get off, but Kristy gently pushed her back down. "Remember? You promised to stay on the four-wheeler."

"It's an apartment," Julie explained. "Apparently they planned to hire someone to live here and look after the place."

"It has a bathroom and a little kitchen," Carrie said. "Rosie and I could live in there!"

Julie slid the door of the closest stall open. "There are automatic waterers in every stall. No more carrying heavy water buckets."

"What?" Rosie turned around. "What's an automatic waterer?"

Jared, Julie's son, snickered, as if everyone ought to know what an automatic waterer was. Rosie elbowed him. Jared was a few weeks younger than Rosie, but since he was the oldest in his family and the only boy of all the cousins, he often acted as if he were older, and smarter, than Rosie.

Julie pointed to a tall silver cylinder in the corner of the stall. "I don't know exactly how it works myself, but from what I understand there's a balance system. When it's full the system is balanced and no more water flows in. As the horse drinks, the bucket becomes lighter and the change in weight triggers something that causes water to flow into the bucket. It also has a heater so the water doesn't freeze in the winter."

Rosie studied her aunt to see whether she was kidding or not. "Can they get chocolate milk out of that thing too?"

Carrie went over to investigate. "Scamper would like that."

"Afraid not," Julie laughed. "Just water, but it does measure how much the horse drinks each day."

Rosie shook her head in disbelief.

"Come on, let's show them the woods," Jonathan suggested. He and Julie led the way back down the aisle and around the front of the barn into what had at one time been a pasture. Now it was a massive tangle of burrs, thistles, and thorn bushes.

"It's like a jungle." Rosie pushed aside the prickly weeds in front of her. "This stuff is taller than my head."

"The weeds are out of control," Jonathan agreed. "It just needs to be mowed a few times."

"Out of my way kids." Grandma steered the four-wheeler around everyone to the front of the line. She turned and pointed behind her to the two flattened paths created by her wheels. "Aren't you glad you brought me along?"

The kids and adults stepped into the paths and continued across the field.

16

"There's plenty of room for pasture for the horses, and we can set aside some of the land as a hay field so we can bale our own hay," Jonathan said.

"This is the best part of the property." Julie waved her hand toward the trees at the edge of the woods. The maple, oak, and hickory trees were in various stages of fall foliage. Sunlight streamed through the treetops highlighting the yellow, orange and bright red leaves. "There's about seventy acres of woods back here."

"It's beautiful," Grandma said.

Rosie turned a complete circle. "We could have some cool trails in here."

"Come on." Jared motioned to the girls. "I picked out a tree where I'm going to build a tree house. Wait till you see it!"

The cousins took off after Jared, laughing and racing through the woods.

"Okay," Eric admitted. "The barn and land are impressive, but we still need a place to live. I can't agree to buy anything until I see what the inside of that house looks like."

"Where's your pioneer spirit?" Julie laughed.

"Easy for you to say. You have a comfortable house to live in." Eric started toward the house, and the adults followed.

"Mom, why don't you stay with the kids?" Kristy suggested. "I don't think that four-wheeler will make it through the front door."

"Okay. Let me know what you find." Grandma turned the four-wheeler around and headed back into the woods.

As they got closer to the house, the weeds became thicker and thorny bushes grabbed at their pant legs. Eric stopped and eyed the dilapidated porch. "I think we'd better use the back door. That porch doesn't look safe."

Jonathan led the way. The back of the house looked even worse than the front. Vines grew up the faded wooden walls and into the windows where several panes had fallen out. Jonathan turned the knob of the back door and pushed, but the door didn't budge. "Hmm. I know this opens. I was just in here the other day." He backed up a step and slammed his shoulder against the door. It popped open with a horrible screech, and he and Eric stepped inside. Julie and Kristy peeked in and looked around the room, then followed the men.

Kristy stared at the wallpaper hanging from the walls in strips. In many places the plaster had fallen off, leaving the wooden wall slats exposed like a skeleton. She accidentally kicked a pile of trash on the kitchen floor. Something small and furry skittered over her shoe. She yelled and ran back to the door.

"It's only a mouse," Eric said.

"You expect me to live here? With mice?"

I have one word for that, Eric said. "June Bug."

Kristy frowned. "That's two words."

"Okay, two. How many mice do you think will be brave enough to stay in this house if we bring that wildcat over here?"

Kristy thought about Grandma's ferocious little bob-tailed cat. "Well—none, I guess." She crept back across the kitchen.

Eric and Jonathan wandered from room to room examining windows, doors, and wiring. There were two large stairways—one at each end of the house, with elaborately carved wooden banisters. Two of the rooms on the second floor had fireplaces. Under all the dirt and trash, they discovered beautiful hardwood floors.

"This must have been a grand house at one time." Eric looked up eyeing the beams visible through holes in the crumbling ceiling. "The underlying structure seems solid. They don't make beams like that anymore, but," he shook his head, "it's going to take a lot of work to make this livable again."

Rosie had reached the top of the stairs in time to hear the last of her father's comments. "We'll help!"

The rest of the kids ran up after her. "Yeah, we'll all help," Jared agreed. Carrie and the twins nodded enthusiastically.

Thump. Thump. Thump. Grandma's crutches bumped up the stairs. She smiled triumphantly when she reached the top.

19

"It looks quite homey to me." Tick ran around her, stopping to sniff through each pile of trash.

"Mom! What are you doing?" Kristy scolded. "You shouldn't be going up and down stairs yet."

"I had to see what we're buying, didn't I?"

Rosie gasped. "You mean we really are going to buy it?"

One by one the adults began to smile.

"Let's do it," Grandma said.

# Chapter 3

# Creation Research

"Hast thou given the horse strength? Hast thou clothed his neck with thunder?" Grandma read aloud from her laptop screen as the girls entered her room. They had just finished a quick ride after returning from looking at the farm. Carrie sat down on the edge of the bed.

Rosie plopped onto the floor and pulled off her boots. She tossed them aside and dragged a wooden rocking chair up beside Grandma. "What's that from?"

"Job 39:19. I searched for all the verses that mention horses in the Bible. There are over one hundred, but that's my favorite."

"What does it mean?" Carrie asked.

"One of the main points of the book of Job is how we can't begin to understand how God created all the amazing things in our world—the sun, stars, plants, animals, people. God asked Job question after question about creation. 'Where wast thou when I laid the foundations of the earth? Declare, if thou hast understanding.'[1]"

---

[1] Job 38:4

Grandma grew quiet and stared out the window. "Think about it. We're spinning around at one thousand miles per hour on a big ball that is precisely the right distance from the sun for our existence. Any closer and we would burn up. A little further away and we'd freeze. I'll never understand how anyone can believe that happened by accident."

Rosie scrunched her face up. "But what does 'clothed his neck with thunder' mean?"

Grandma switched the screen to the web browser and turned the laptop around. "Look at this."

Rosie moved closer so she could see the photo of a large black horse. "A Friesian! That's one of my favorite breeds."

"Look at the arch of his neck with that long, flowing mane. That's the picture I get when I think of a neck clothed with thunder," Grandma said. "Or a wild stallion prancing around protecting his herd. 'Clothed with thunder' seems to symbolize the horse's power and strength, but also his beauty."

Rosie smiled. "Kind of like Scamper."

Carrie and Grandma looked at each other and rolled their eyes. "Yeah, right," Carrie laughed.

Rosie pulled a notebook and pen out of her backpack. "All right, let's get to work. Where do we start?"

"About sixty million years ago," Carrie said. "According to Emily."

Rosie turned to her grandmother. "How does anyone know what happened millions of years ago? A million years is a long time."

"That's the problem," Grandma said. "No one does. Both sides of the argument require faith. Creationists put their faith in God and the Bible, while the evolutionists' faith is in scientific theories."

Rosie knew this was one of Grandma's favorite topics. Since they were often outside together with the horses, she and Carrie were always learning things about creation from their grandmother. Just the other day she had been explaining how the process of photosynthesis affected when it was safe to let Scamper out to graze[2].

Rosie had never even heard of photosynthesis before. Later when she put Scamper in his stall, she tried to explain the whole process to him, but he didn't seem terribly interested.

Rosie thought one of the most amazing things God created was the Monarch butterfly. She couldn't believe how many different forms it took—beginning as an egg, then turning into a caterpillar, forming a chrysalis and finally emerging as a beautiful butterfly. Some of those butterflies would later fly up to three thousand miles to Mexico to join millions of other Monarchs for the winter.

---

[2] Through the process of photosynthesis, plants convert light, water and carbon dioxide into sugar, which is stored in the plant. Overnight, when there is no light, the sugar levels in grass decrease; therefore horses that are susceptible to founder/laminitis can graze most safely in the early morning hours before the sugar levels begin building up again.

Grandma set the laptop down and looked at the girls. "Maybe you should talk about irreducible complexity."

"Irre-what?" Carrie repeated.

"*Irreducible* means that something can't be reduced or broken apart. Irreducible complexity stumps evolutionists, but fits perfectly with God as Creator."

"What is it?" Rosie asked.

"Remember when I was hurt on the trail ride?"

"Grandma, that was only a week ago. Of course I remember."

Carrie nodded. "I won't ever forget that day."

Grandma held up her arm. "My arm was cut pretty badly." She straightened the bandage and winced. "Think about what happened. Why did your mom tear up your shirt and press it on my arm?"

Rosie thought that was obvious. "To stop the bleeding."

"But why did it stop? Why didn't it start bleeding again as soon as she stopped pressing on it?"

Grandma was always asking "why" questions to find out whether her grandchildren really understood things. While Rosie was trying to remember some of the science she had studied, Carrie piped up, "Blood clots?"

"Right!" Grandma nodded. "When my arm was cut, that started a whole chain of processes in my body."

Rosie put her notebook down and leaned back in the rocker. She knew that once her grandmother got started on a topic like this, there was no stopping her.

"I don't know all the details, but this is what I understand. When you cut yourself, blood starts flowing out of the wound. There are little things that float around in our blood called *platelets*. Something in our bodies signals the platelets to start sticking to the wound."

Grandma paused. "Some other things happen, and then these sticky threads made of something called *fibrin* criss-cross over the platelets to form a mass that blocks off the opening of the cut and stops the bleeding—a clot or scab."

"The same thing happened when Kezzie cut her leg?" Carrie asked.

"Exactly."

"And the irreducible complexity part?" Rosie reminded her.

"There's a lot more to it. I'm certainly no expert. I know there are red and white blood cells, proteins, and enzymes. You could ask your Aunt Lisa. She studied all that in nursing school. But yes, the irreducible complexity part—all these things work together. If any part of the system doesn't work, the blood doesn't clot. And if the blood doesn't clot, the person or animal will bleed to death from even a small scratch."

"I get it," Carrie said. "So everyone would have bled to death while they were waiting for all the parts of the blood clotting process to evolve."

"It would seem so," Grandma said. "Although, if you're an evolutionist, you'd have to wonder how life and cells and blood and everything else came about in the first place. Do you know there may be as many as one hundred trillion cells in the human body? And inside each of those cells are. . ."

Rosie picked up her notebook and waved it around. "Um, Grandma, our demonstration?"

"Oh, right." Grandma turned back to the computer. "Now, what's the name of the first little critter you want me to look up?"

"I guess Eohippus," Carrie said. "That's the one Emily started with."

Rosie carefully printed the name in her notebook.

"E-o-hippus," Grandma repeated slowly as she typed the name into the computer. "Here we go." An article with images of several animals of various sizes appeared on the screen. Grandma turned the laptop so the girls could see it. "Why don't you read it out loud, Carrie?"

Several hours later the door creaked open, and Kristy peeked into the room. The girls were sitting on each side of Grandma on the bed, all three focused on the computer in front of them. "Can you take a break long enough to eat dinner?"

Grandma looked up. "Is it that late already?"

"It's 6:30. I've got dinner ready. Eric's here." The smell of baked chicken drifted through the open bedroom door.

The girls jumped off the bed. "Now that you mention it, I'm as hungry as a horse," Rosie said.

They took their seats around the kitchen table, joined hands, and prayed. Eric passed the potatoes to Rosie. "How's the research going?"

"Grandma helped us find a lot of information." Rosie held up her notebook. "I have about ten pages of notes already."

"How are you going to present it?" Kristy asked.

Rosie looked puzzled. "What do you mean? We'll just. . . you know. . . give a demonstration."

"Since the beginning of time all 4-H demonstrations have always been the same. The kids hold up a poster and talk or read something," Kristy said. "Don't you think you could be a little more creative? After all this is a demonstration on creation."

"Yeah, a lot of the demonstrations are boring," Carrie agreed. "Sometimes I can't even hear what they're saying or see the tiny pictures on their posters."

"I know!" Rosie pushed her chair back and began walking around the table. "I could be an archeologist who discovers a fossil that I think proves the evolution of the horse." She stopped and put her hand on Carrie's head. "And you could be a TV reporter interviewing me about it."

Carrie twisted around to look at her. "You mean we would act it out? Like a play?"

Rosie smiled and nodded. "Do you want to?" she asked eagerly.

"I guess so—but if you find a fossil that supports evolution, how is that going to convince people to believe in creation?"

"You'll see." Rosie smiled and sat back down. "This is going to take a lot of work. What about our schoolwork, Mom? We didn't do any today."

Kristy laughed. "Homeschooling is about learning, not doing 'schoolwork.' Today you learned about research, science, debate, writing, and the Bible. I'd call that a good day."

"And, so you don't miss out on arithmetic, I have a math problem for you," Eric added.

Carrie frowned. "Aw, couldn't we just take a break from math for a while?"

Eric shook his head. "Nope, you're not getting off that easy. This is a story problem. If we sell our house for $100,000, and Grandma sells her place for $175,000, how much can we afford to pay for the new farm?"

Rosie opened her notebook and started writing down numbers.

"Grandma doesn't owe anything on her house," Eric continued, "but we have a mortgage we'll have to pay off when our house sells—about $60,000. We'll also need to have enough money left over for repairs on the new farm house."

"We could board some horses to help with expenses," Grandma suggested.

Eric nodded. "I was thinking that too. Figure out how many stalls we'll need for our horses, how many Julie will use, and how many that will leave for boarders."

"You'll have to determine what we could charge for board and what expenses we'll have," Kristy joined in.

"Whoa!" Rosie sighed and dropped the pen onto her notebook. "You're going too fast. I can't write all this down."

Mortgages and the cost of house repairs were a mystery to her. She was confident her dad would figure all that out. She leaned back and smiled, imagining herself on Scamper leading a group of happy campers on a trail ride through the woods.

# Chapter 4

# The Farrier

"This is Carrie Jackson, roving reporter for KZN News. Have you made any important discoveries in that stall today?" Carrie shoved the curry comb she was using for a microphone into Rosie's face.

"Um, no more than usual." Rosie tossed a pitchfork full of manure into the wheelbarrow and looked at Carrie as if she had lost her mind.

Carrie peered into the wheelbarrow. "Any idea how old this discovery is? What are you using—carbon dating or the potassium argon method?" She shifted the curry comb back toward her sister.

Rosie rolled her eyes. "I'm glad you're getting into your role as a TV reporter, but we need to get these stalls clean before the farrier gets here."

"Oh, all right. I just want to do a good job on our demonstration, so I thought I'd start practicing." Carrie exchanged her microphone for a pitchfork. As they emptied the last load, Tick began barking ferociously at a bright red pickup truck pulling down the lane.

"Dean's here." Rosie ran to catch the pup. Tick was running back and forth in front of the truck. Rosie slipped her hand through the dog's collar and ran back to the barn with her.

Carrie found a lead rope and tied Tick to a post. The puppy ran after her. When she hit the end of the rope, she nearly did a flip, then got back on all four feet and yapped loudly, struggling to free herself.

Carrie walked backwards away from Tick, pointing her finger at the pup. "Stay," she said in her gruffest voice. She bumped into Rosie and turned around. "I thought Aunt Julie was coming to handle Sassy."

Rosie nodded. "She'll be here. At least, I hope so. She's supposed to take Sassy home with her today."

"Aw, our horses will be so disappointed that Sassy is leaving," Carrie laughed.

Dean opened the side panel of the truck bed, and gathered his tools. "Good morning girls. How's your grandmother?"

"Much better," Rosie replied. "She's getting around pretty well on her crutches now."

"Here she comes!" Carrie pointed toward the house where Grandma was opening the back gate.

"What's this I hear about a new resident of Sonrise Stable?"

"Her name is Sassy," Carrie said.

"She's a mule," Rosie added.

"So I hear. It's been a while since I've had any long-ears on my roster."

"Hi Dean." Grandma leaned her crutches against the barn wall and stopped to catch her breath.

"You're looking good. I expect you'll be back in the saddle before long, won't you?"

Grandma laughed. "I better wait until this cast comes off. They promised me it will only be another three weeks."

Dean looked around. "Who are we doing first today?"

"Julie's going to hold Sassy. She should be here any minute," Grandma said. "Carrie, why don't you get Zach?"

Carrie ran to her horse's stall, snapped a lead rope onto his halter, and led the palomino gelding to the front of the barn.

"Zach?" Dean raised his eyebrows. "Isn't this Bandit?" He looked at the horse more closely. "It is Bandit. What are you doing here, buddy?"

"Bandit? How did you know that was his name?" Rosie asked. "Carrie changed his name to Zacheaus, but we call him Zach."

"I've trimmed Bandit for years."

"My son-in-law bought him for Carrie during the fair," Grandma explained.

"Yeah," Rosie hissed, "from that rat, Billy King."

Grandma frowned at her. "Shhh."

33

Dean pulled the hoof nippers out of his box. "Yes, the Kings live not far from Julie's place."

"Oh no," Rosie whispered to Carrie. "He'll be close to our new farm. We'll have to watch out. He might try to steal Bandit."

Carrie's eyes grew wide. "Zach, you mean."

"Yeah. You know what I mean. We'll have to be careful."

Carrie nodded and looked out toward the road. "Here comes Aunt Julie."

Julie pulled in and parked her truck and trailer beside Dean's. She opened her trailer door, then walked to the barn.

"Where are the kids?" Grandma asked as Julie reached them.

"Finishing up barn chores. We had to do some rearranging to make room for Sassy."

Dean ran his hand down Zach's shoulder, picked up his front hoof and began trimming.

Carrie poked her elbow into Rosie's side and whispered, "Ask him about evolution."

"No, you ask him," Rosie whispered back.

Carrie shook her head firmly and took a step back.

Rosie put her hands on her hips and sighed. She couldn't understand why Carrie was still so shy around some people.

"Dean, do you think horses could have eighteen ribs, then fifteen, then nineteen, then back to eighteen[3] again?"

Dean set Zach's foot down, stood up and looked at Rosie. "Is this a riddle?"

Rosie shook her head. "No. Carrie and I are going to do a demonstration for our 4-H club to show them that horses couldn't have evolved."

"Well. . ." Dean scratched his head. "Most horses have eighteen pairs of ribs, but sometimes Arabians have seventeen, and I have heard of horses that have nineteen."

Rosie thought for a moment. If she could figure out a way to convince Dean, it might work with the kids in her 4-H club also. "Grandma says anything that looks like it was designed must have had a designer. She says that a horse's hooves were designed perfectly for the horse."

"She's got a good point there. Hey, hang on a second." Dean trotted out to his truck.

Rosie watched as he pulled something out of a compartment in the back of his truck and headed back to the barn. "What is that? It looks like a horse's leg."

Carrie squirmed. "Eww!"

Dean waved the leg, an actual horse's leg that had been preserved, in front of them. "Don't worry, it's not alive." He turned the leg upside down and pointed to the bottom of the

---

[3] Eohippus (18), Orohippus (15), Pliohippus (19), Horse (18)

hoof. "Of course you know this is the sole and the frog. Do you know what the frog does?"

"It catches a lot of mud that I have to clean out of Scamper's hooves," Rosie laughed.

"Technically that's not the frog, but the grooves on each side of the frog." The leg had been sawn down the middle and hinged at the back. Dean unfastened a snap and opened it.

Rosie moved closer so she could see the inside of the leg. Carrie took one look and started to turn pale.

"The frog, along with the digital cushion," Dean pointed to a padded area inside the hoof above the frog, "serve as shock absorbers. That makes it easier on your horse's legs—like the shocks in your car. And, every time the horse takes a step, the frog helps pump blood back up his leg."

Rosie pointed. "What's this? I didn't know there was a bone inside their hoof."

"That's the coffin bone. The hoof wall is attached to the coffin bone by tissues called *lamina* that contain blood vessels and nerves. When a horse founders, the lamina are damaged and no longer hold the wall to the bone as tightly. The coffin bone can rotate downward and may pop out through the sole of the foot. In fact, in the worst cases the hoof falls right off."

Rosie grimaced.

"Ew, ew, ew!" Carrie pressed the palms of her hands over both ears and shut her eyes tightly.

Dean glanced at Carrie, then turned to Grandma. "Maybe that was a little too much information?"

Grandma smiled grimly and nodded.

"Ah." Dean snapped the horse leg shut, set it off to the side, and went back to trimming Zach.

Rosie nudged Carrie. She dropped her hands and opened one eye.

"It's safe," Rosie assured her. "He doesn't have the leg anymore."

Julie laughed. "I take it you don't want to be a nurse like your Aunt Lisa?"

Carrie shook her head. "Definitely not. I'm going to be a writer."

Rosie walked around to watch Dean. "Evolutionists think chestnuts[4] are what used to be one of the horse's toes."

Dean laughed. "That's a funny place for a toe. Interesting that you bring that up. Chestnuts are sort of like our fingerprints—uniquely identifying each horse. I was also reading something the other day that said they may have a scent function. They're totally within the skin, not connected to bone at all, so I don't see how they could be an old toe. Just because we don't know what function a body part has, doesn't mean it doesn't have one. Scientists used to believe our appendix had no purpose, but recently they've discovered that it stores good bacteria until it's needed by our intestines."

"So, you don't believe in evolution?" Rosie asked.

---

[4] Small oval areas of horny tissue at knee level on the inside of a horse's front and back legs

"I don't know." Dean shrugged. "I've never given it much thought."

"Will you still trim our horses when we move to the new farm?" Rosie asked.

Dean set Zach's hoof down. "What? You're moving?"

Grandma frowned. "Now, Rosie, how many times have I warned you about that? It's not our farm yet and might never be."

"We're trying to buy a farm out past my house that's going up for auction," Julie said.

"Oh, the old Carter place," Dean said. "Beautiful barn, but the house is falling apart."

Julie nodded. "If we get it, we're counting on my husband and the girls' dad to fix it up."

Carrie led Zach back to his stall, and Rosie hurried to get Scamper. "Your turn, now, Scamp." As Dean worked on her pony, Rosie chattered away, filling him in on all the details about the new farm.

Julie led Sassy up next. "Her feet are in pretty bad shape. I haven't ridden her much yet. I didn't want to make them any worse."

She positioned the mule in the aisle, and Dean examined the dry, brittle hooves that had large chunks broken out of them. "That's unusual. Generally mules have hooves like iron. What was her mother?"

"A Quarter Horse, I think," Julie replied.

"She seems to have inherited her hooves from her mother's side of the family. I'll straighten them up, then you can try some hoof boots if you're going to ride her much. That should keep them from chipping more while they're growing out. I don't want to shoe her unless I have to."

"Aw, she's going to have baby booties," Rosie laughed.

"Speaking of babies," Grandma said, "did you girls know mules can't have them?"

Dean nodded. "Sassy's father, a donkey, has sixty-two chromosomes, and her mother, a horse, has sixty-four. Mules are born with sixty-three."

Rosie smiled mischievously. "I knew there was something a little odd about her."

"Poor Sassy." Julie rubbed the mule's forehead. "Don't you listen to her."

"Actually I did hear of one case of a mule having a foal,[5]" Dean said, "but it's extremely rare. You might be able to tie that in to your demonstration. If it's so difficult for the offspring of two closely related animals to reproduce, that doesn't say much for the possibility of Eohippus randomly turning into a horse—or monkeys evolving into humans, for that matter."

"That's a good idea," Rosie agreed. "I hadn't thought about that."

---

[5] Kate, a mule owned by Larry and Laura Amos in Colbran, CO gave birth to a mule foal in April of 2007. Genetic testing at the University of California, Davis confirmed that the mule was indeed the foal's mother.

When Dean finished Sassy, he looked around the barn. "Are we doing Kezzie today?"

"Let's wait until next time," Grandma said. "She's still not putting her full weight on the injured leg."

Dean nodded and began packing his tools away.

Julie tapped Rosie's shoulder. "Can you lead Scamper out to my trailer?"

Rosie gulped. "You're not taking my horse, are you? I thought you were taking Sassy."

"No, I'm not going to take your horse. I figured I'd need a little help getting this mule in the trailer."

"Oh. Okay. Come on, Scamp." Rosie followed Julie as she started toward the trailer with Sassy.

The mule jumped into the trailer and turned her head, expecting Scamper to follow right behind her. Julie unfastened the lead and quickly closed the door. "Sorry to trick you, girl. You'll make some new friends at my place and who knows? Maybe you'll be reunited with your beloved Kezzie soon at the new farm."

Sassy peeked through the window at Scamper. She brayed loudly, pawing and banging against the sides of the trailer. Julie waved and hurried into her truck. "Bye everyone. I need to get moving before she destroys my trailer."

Rosie and Scamper turned and headed back to the barn. "You won't miss old Mule Head will you, buddy? I know Kezzie won't."

Grandma wrote out a check and handed it to Dean.

"Thanks. I've got you down for your next appointment in eight weeks."

"You aren't leaving *that*," Carrie pointed toward the preserved horse leg on the barn floor, "are you?"

Dean picked the leg up and offered it to Carrie. "Do you want to use it for your demonstration?"

Carrie jumped back and shook her head. Dean smiled and tucked the leg under his arm. He gathered the rest of his equipment and started toward his truck.

"Dean," Rosie said.

He stopped and looked back. "Yes?"

"Don't forget, we'll be at the new farm next time."

"Gotcha," Dean laughed.

# Chapter 5

# Farm Finances

Eric dropped a stack of papers onto the kitchen table and pulled out a chair. "Okay, girls, tomorrow's the big day. Let's see what kind of figures you came up with."

Carrie ran to get the paper she and Rosie had been working on all week and held it out to Rosie.

Rosie pushed it back. "You do the first part."

The girls sat down side by side at the table. Carrie set the paper in front of her and pointed to a sketch Rosie had drawn of the new barn. "We thought we'd keep our horses here." Carrie counted them off on her fingers. "Zach, Scamper, Kezzie, Sassy—and Scout, Patches, and Pearl in the far left row of stalls. That's seven horses and seven stalls. Julie can have six stalls on the other side of the aisle for the horses she's training. That leaves the first stall for a tack room."

Eric nodded. "Sounds like a good plan."

"The other side of the barn is for the boarders," Rosie continued. "There are fourteen stalls on that side too. Carrie and I figured we could charge $400 a month for each horse, so let me see. . ." Rosie searched the paper for the total she had written down. "Here it is. That's $5,600 each month, $67,200 a year! We'll be rich!"

Eric smiled and thumbed through his papers. "Aren't you forgetting a few things?"

Rosie and Carrie looked at their paper, then at each other. "What, Dad?" Rosie asked.

Grandma and Kristy joined them at the table. "Those horses might need something to eat," Kristy said.

"I thought Uncle Jonathan said we were going to grow our own hay," Rosie said.

"Yes, but there will still be expenses involved—keeping the tractor running, fuel, baling twine, and other supplies."

"Oh," Rosie said. "I didn't think about that."

"We'll need to feed them some grain too," Grandma reminded the girls.

"Except for Scamper," Carrie laughed. "He's too fat already."

"At least he'll save us money," Rosie sniffed. "Oh yeah, we forgot about bedding."

Eric picked up the girls' paper and read it over. "This looks good, except we can't use all fourteen of those stalls for boarders. We'll need one for another tack room. That way the boarders won't have to come over to the family side of the barn."

Rosie and Carrie nodded. "And," Eric pointed to the drawing, "I thought I could turn this area into a small lounge with a restroom."

"I've been wondering," Grandma said. "It's a great facility with the indoor arena, and the property is beautiful, but it's out in the middle of nowhere. Do you think we'll be able to attract many boarders?"

Kristy nodded. "That's a good point. It would be a long drive for most people."

"But they'll love it when they see it," Rosie said.

"Yes, I'm sure they will," Grandma agreed, "but boarders generally want something convenient, too."

Eric frowned. "It would make a serious dent in our income if we don't fill the boarder side of the barn."

"Oh!" Carrie leaned forward on the edge of her seat and waved her hand in the air. "I know!"

They all turned to look at her.

"What?" Rosie asked.

"Oh, never mind." Carrie sat back. "It probably wouldn't work."

"No, go ahead and tell us, honey," Kristy urged. "We could use some ideas."

"I was thinking about how much fun Cousins Camp was. What if we had horse camps like that for kids in the summer?"

"That's a great idea!" Rosie clapped Carrie on the shoulder. "Isn't it, Mom, Dad? Grandma?"

"You may be on to something," Grandma said. "We might be able to make as much doing that for two or three months each summer as we could with boarding year 'round."

"That reminds me." Eric jotted a note on one of his papers. "Add liability insurance to our list of expenses. And if we do have boarders, you kids are going to be the stall cleaning crew."

"You can teach me how to drive Uncle Jonathan's tractor," Rosie said. "That would be a lot easier than using a wheelbarrow."

"I'll drive the tractor, and you can clean the stalls," Carrie said.

Rosie started doodling on the paper. "Yeah, right. You would crash it into the barn."

"Okay girls." Eric held up his hand like a referee. "Why don't we wait and see if we even get the place before you start arguing about who's going to do what." He laid the papers down and crossed his arms. "I calculated what our monthly payments would be for different prices, and we can afford to go as high as $300,000 for the farm, but not a penny more."

Rosie dropped her pencil and stared. Her dad might as well have said three million dollars as far as she was concerned. She had never imagined they could afford anything that expensive. Surely no one else would be able to pay that much.

"That leaves room for the repairs on the house," he continued. "If we can get some boarders or the summer camp idea works out, I think we could have the loan paid off in ten years."

"How many people do you think will be there tomorrow?" Kristy asked.

Eric shrugged. "I have no idea. The barn and property are certainly appealing, but I'm sure that house will scare a lot of people away."

Rosie slapped her hand on the table. "I think it will scare all of them away." She looked over at her dad. "Are we done now?"

Eric nodded.

Rosie hopped up and started out of the kitchen, then turned around and held up her hand. "Don't go anywhere. I want to show you guys something." She ran through the living room and up the stairs.

Eric turned to Carrie. "What's this all about?"

"It's a surprise," Carrie said mysteriously. "I'm not supposed to tell."

Rosie returned in a few minutes with her sketch pad. She set the tablet down on the table and flipped through it. When she located the page she was looking for, she turned it around so everyone could see the colored pencil drawing. A bay Arabian with flowing mane and tail was nose to nose with a short doglike creature.

"Rosie, that horse is beautiful," Grandma said. "You are becoming quite the artist."

47

"But what is this?" Eric pointed to the small brown creature on the right.

"It's an Eohippus, Dad. The horse is staring at it wondering how in the world anyone could think that he evolved from that ugly little thing."

"Ah, I get it." Eric nodded.

Rosie held the drawing up in front of her. "Could we get T-shirts made from it? Carrie and I thought it would be cool to wear them when we do our demonstration." Rosie looked around the table at her parents and grandmother.

"I don't see why not," Kristy said. "They make transfer paper so you can print the design from the computer and then iron it on. That should work for just two shirts."

"Do you think the shirt should say something?" Grandma said. "People might think you mean the horse *did* evolve from Eohippus."

Rosie frowned. "Oh, I hadn't thought about that."

"What about Genesis 1:25 where it says that God made the beasts of the earth after their kind?" Grandma suggested.

"I don't know," Kristy said. "Some people might still misinterpret it. They might think it means that God used evolution to make the horse from the Eohippus."

"I know!" Carrie said. "What if we add a speech bubble and have the horse saying, 'Grandpa?'"

Rosie smiled. "Funny, but they might still get the wrong idea."

"What about adding a P.S. after the Bible verse?" Eric said. "Like, 'P.S. He did it in one day!'"

"Then they'll say one day is like a thousand—or a million years," Grandma said.

Rosie groaned. "What about: God created the horse on the sixth day—that is one day, not thousands or millions of years—and He didn't use evolution!"

"That's pretty clear all right," Grandma laughed, "but I'm not sure you could fit it all on a shirt."

"I like the P.S. idea," Carrie said.

Rosie nodded. "Me too."

"I think it's perfect," Kristy agreed. "If you're finished with the drawing, I'll scan it tomorrow and add the text. Then we'll have to run into town and pick up the paper and shirts."

"I want to add a little more color and shading to the horse, but I can finish it tonight." Rosie closed the sketch pad and smiled. This was going to be a great demonstration.

# Chapter 6

# The Auction

"There it is!" Rosie bounced in the back seat as they turned into the driveway of the farm property early the next morning. She pointed to a spot at the end of the drive. "We can put the Sonrise Stable sign right there so everyone will see it when they drive by."

Kristy laughed. "Like a lot of people drive by here."

Rosie scanned the driveway and the weed-covered front yard and smiled. "There aren't many people here. I guess the house did scare them away."

"We're early. I'm sure more people will show up later." Eric pulled the car off the side of the driveway.

The auctioneer was setting up a microphone and loudspeaker in a hay wagon between the house and the barn. A few people were standing around chatting or taking a last look at the property.

"There's Julie and Jonathan and the kids." Grandma adjusted her crutches and waved to catch their attention.

Julie walked over wearing a strained expression on her usually smiling face. "I'm so nervous I can hardly breathe." She stopped and took in a deep breath. Jessie and Jamie followed her, powdered sugar all over their mouths and donuts in their hands.

Jared looked over at his sisters and shook his head. "You two are a mess."

"They're fine," Jonathan said. "Eric, why don't you do the bidding?"

"Sure." Eric turned to Rosie and Carrie. "Keep still once the auction starts. If you so much as scratch your nose the auctioneer might think you're placing a bid."

Rosie nodded and glanced nervously at the auctioneer. More trucks and cars pulled in. Soon the driveway was lined with vehicles all the way out to the road. *Why did all these people have to show up?*

"Oh, girls," Kristy said. "I had a thought about your demonstration. Remember when we were on the trail ride, and Kezzie spotted the turkeys off in the distance?"

Rosie nodded. "Everyone saw them, except Grandma."

"Hey, don't make fun of old people," Grandma said.

"Maybe you could talk a little about horses' eyes," Kristy said.

"What's so special about their eyes?" Carrie asked.

"Horses have the largest eyes of any land animal," Julie said, "and they can see almost all the way around their bodies, except for small blind spots directly in front of and behind them."

"Remember when we were little, how we thought Mom must have had eyes in the back of her head?" Kristy laughed. "She seemed to know what we were doing no matter where we were."

"If evolution were true, mothers would have three arms and about six eyes." Grandma smiled. "You know—survival of the fittest."

Julie laughed. "Okay, back to the demonstration. Horses have both monocular and binocular vision. They can see with one eye on each side and with both eyes in front of them. They see in color too."

"They also have better distance and night vision than people do," Grandma added.

"I should have brought my notebook," Rosie said. "I'll never remember all this."

"Let's get started," the auctioneer called out. He paused until the crowd had gathered around and everyone was quiet. "We have for sale a parcel of one hundred acres which includes the barn you see on my left." He pointed toward the stable, and the crowd all looked in that direction.

"And the house on the right." The auctioneer motioned to his right and quickly continued, as if he didn't want the people to look too long at the house. "The property is selling as-is, with no warranty of any kind; ten percent down payment due within a week of the close of the sale."

Rosie shifted nervously from foot to foot. *Please, God, help us get the farm.*

"Okay, who'll start us out? How about $200,000?"

The crowd looked up at the auctioneer, but remained silent.

"Look at this acreage, folks—brand-spanking new stable, seventy wooded acres. Who'll give me $150,000?" The auctioneer began to chant in a sing-song voice.

Rosie scanned the crowd and noticed a man with a long gray beard off to her right nod slightly.

"Okay, I've got one-fifty, who'll give me one-sixty? One-sixty, one-sixty, who'll give me one-sixty?"

An older woman in a red jacket raised her hand.

"Yes! I've got one-sixty. How about one-seventy?"

Eric didn't move a muscle. Rosie stared at her dad in disbelief. "Why aren't you bidding, Dad? They're going to take our farm!"

Kristy put both her hands on Rosie's shoulders and leaned over until her face was close to Rosie's ear. "Shh! Your dad has done this before. He knows what he's doing."

Grandma twisted the rolled-up sale flyer back and forth in her hands and smiled nervously at Rosie.

The bidding continued back and forth between a handful of people, the auctioneer chanting rapidly in what sounded like a foreign language.

"What in the world is he saying?" Carrie whispered to Rosie.

She shrugged her shoulders. "I'm not sure. I think they might be at $240,000 now."

"Two-fifty," Eric called out.

Rosie smiled at Carrie and pumped her fist in the air. "Yes!"

Everyone turned to look at Eric. The auctioneer paused for a moment. "A new face." He smiled and resumed his chant. "Okay now, who'll give me two-sixty?" He looked to the woman in red, but she stared at the ground, shaking her head. However, the bearded man gave a quick nod.

"Two-seventy," the auctioneer requested.

Eric nodded.

"I've got Two-seventy, who'll give me two-eighty?"

The other man bid again.

The only thing holding Rosie on the ground was her mother's hands on her shoulders. *We almost have it! Please God, make him stop bidding.*

The auctioneer turned back to Eric. "Two-ninety?"

Eric raised his hand to place the bid. Rosie held her breath as the auctioneer turned back to the other bidder. The man hesitated. Rosie stared intently at him. *No, don't bid on our farm.*

"I've got two-ninety. Will anyone give me three hundred? It's a great deal for this fine property." The auctioneer looked out over the crowd to see whether anyone else was willing to jump in this late in the sale. He turned to the other man one last time and paused.

Rosie watched in horror as the man slowly nodded his head.

"No, you can't. It's our farm."

"Hush, Rosie," Kristy tried to put her arm around her, but Rosie pulled away.

"I've got three hundred. Now I need three-ten." The auctioneer droned on.

No one responded.

He turned to look at Eric again. "Can you go three-oh-five?"

"Dad, can't you bid one more time?" Rosie begged. "It's only five thousand more."

Eric looked drained, as if he had just finished running a marathon. "No, Rosie. I'm sorry. We can't afford it."

"Going once, going twice. . ." The auctioneer paused and looked over the crowd one last time. "Gone!" he announced. "To this gentleman over here."

Rosie stared in stunned silence as the top bidder walked up to the auctioneer smiling broadly. She trudged behind the rest of the family back to the car.

Eric put his hand on the door, then turned back to Julie. "I'm sorry. I thought we had it. I didn't think he would go that high."

Julie sniffed and wiped her eyes with the back of her hand. "It's not your fault. I feel kind of numb. I can't believe we didn't get it. Everything about this place seemed like it was perfect for us."

Eric slid into the driver's side and smacked the steering wheel. "I really thought we had it."

Grandma stuck her crutches on the floor of the back seat and sat down. The girls climbed in beside her. Rosie stared out the window. She felt her grandmother patting her leg, but she knew if she looked at anyone, she would burst into tears. It wasn't fair. Now they wouldn't be able to have the summer camps or live down the road from their cousins.

They drove home in silence. When they reached Grandma's house, Rosie ran upstairs to the bedroom and slammed the door. Carrie stood awkwardly in the kitchen.

"Come here, and give me a hug," Grandma said. "I know you must be as disappointed as Rosie."

# Chapter 7

# Creation T-Shirts

Early the next morning Grandma stared at the pancakes on the griddle, watching bubbles form in the yellow dough. She absentmindedly flipped them over, then stacked the perfectly browned cakes on a plate. She set the pancakes in the center of the table and called, "Breakfast is ready!"

One by one the family entered the kitchen and took their seats. Grandma looked around the table. No one was smiling. "I'll pray this morning," she began brightly. "Heavenly Father, we don't always understand Your ways, but we trust that You know what is best for us. Even though we didn't get the farm, You have blessed us in so many other ways—beyond anything we deserve. Bless this food, and help us to always be grateful. Amen."

"Amen," said Rosie softly. She forked a pancake off the plate. "I still don't understand why we didn't get it. We could have had so much fun there."

Grandma shook her head. "I don't understand it either, but I've learned to trust that God's plans are better than mine."

"It's still going to be fun living here with Grandma," Carrie said.

"Yes, and as soon as we sell our house, I can stop flipping back and forth between here and there," Eric added. "We've already had a couple people interested in it."

"How is the demonstration coming?" Kristy asked.

"Okay, I guess," Rosie said. She couldn't muster up much enthusiasm for the project now.

"That reminds me, girls," Eric said. "Looking at that old farmhouse, and actually all the houses I've remodeled over the years, makes me wonder how anyone can believe in evolution."

Rosie stared at her dad blankly. "I don't see the connection."

"What does that house look like now?"

Rosie didn't want to think about the farm any more. She stared at her plate and picked at her food.

"A haunted house?" Carrie offered.

Eric laughed. "Kind of. It's falling apart. Right?" He nudged Rosie, and she nodded.

"What do you think it looked like when it was brand new?"

Rosie shrugged.

"A mansion?" Carrie guessed.

"Maybe. It is one of the largest houses in the area."

Rosie put her fork down and slouched back in her chair. "Dad, what does this have to do with evolution?"

"Houses always fall apart if there isn't anyone to take care of them. I see it all the time. There's some scientific law about that. Oh. . . what's the name?"

"The Second Law of Thermodynamics," Kristy said. "Everything tends to become disordered over time—nothing increases in order or complexity."

"Impressive." Eric smiled.

"I was homeschooled too, you know. And I had a great teacher." Kristy nodded toward Grandma who smiled.

"Anyway," Eric continued. "I thought you girls might be able to use that somehow. If evolution were true, somewhere in the world we should see things improving, but we see the opposite—everything falls apart."

"And, why don't we fall out of bed?" Grandma demanded.

"What?" Her grandmother's question was so unexpected that Rosie had to smile. "What does that have to do with anything?"

"How does an evolutionist explain the fact that we turn over many times while we're sound asleep, but somehow we know where the edge of the bed is and we don't fall out?"

"Or what about dreams?" Kristy said. "There's nothing about dreams that would help a species survive. Why do we dream?"

Rosie turned to Carrie. "Remember when you dreamed about winning the Olympics with Zach?"

Carrie laughed and nodded.

"Another thing that's hard to explain is music," Julie added. "There's such a variety of instruments that can all play the same notes. Music doesn't help people survive. It seems it was designed specifically to bring us pleasure."

"Think about flowers," Kristy said. "All the different kinds—so many colors, shapes, sizes, and smells. What reason is there for flowers to be so beautiful?"

Grandma tipped her head back and got a dreamy look in her eyes. "I can picture God creating one flower after another—and smiling as He painted each of them a different color."

"Speaking of painting," Kristy said, "I picked up the transfers and shirts yesterday. After you two feed the horses, we can work on your T-shirts."

"Okay." Rosie picked up her plate and carried it to the sink. She was still disappointed about the farm, but it would be fun to see her drawing on the shirts. The girls ran to the barn to take care of the animals. When they returned, Kristy had just clicked the print button on the graphics program. The printer buzzed and clicked and started printing.

Rosie's head moved back and forth as she watched the print head travel slowly across the paper. "I can't wait to see how the shirts look."

Kristy got up from the computer desk. "Standing there staring at the printer won't make it print any faster. Why don't you set up the ironing board?"

Rosie walked across the living room to the closet. She pushed a stack of photo albums and a plastic tub full of blankets out of the way in order to get to the rarely-used ironing board. Carrie grabbed the iron off the shelf.

By the time the ironing board was set up and the iron heated, both pages had finished printing. Kristy picked up the package of transfers and read the directions again. She looked at Rosie. "Do you want to do it?"

Rosie shook her head. "I'm afraid I would mess it up. I've never ironed anything in my life. You better do it, Mom."

Rosie and Carrie watched as their mother laid Rosie's shirt on the ironing board and smoothed out the wrinkles. She placed the transfer paper on top and straightened it.

Kristy picked up the iron. "Here goes." She moved it back and forth over the design several times, then set the iron aside.

Rosie crowded next to her trying to see the shirt. "What does it look like, Mom?"

"Be patient. We have to let it cool."

"Let me peel it off," Rosie said. "Tell me when."

After a few minutes Kristy nodded. Rosie grasped the corner of the paper between her thumb and forefinger and carefully pulled it back. "Oh, wow!" She smiled and held the shirt up in front of her. The image was crisp and clear on the light blue shirt. "Hurry up and do Carrie's so we can try them on."

When Carrie's shirt was finished, the girls ran to the bedroom to put them on. They came back arm-in-arm, wearing not only matching shirts, but the same big smile.

Grandma hobbled in from the kitchen. "They look great! Hold on, let me get my camera."

"Stay put. I'll get it." Kristy retrieved the camera from Grandma's room and snapped several photos of the girls. "Okay, you better take them off now so they stay nice for the demonstration next week."

After changing again, Rosie returned with her notebook. She sat down, flipped through the pages and sighed. "Mom, everyone has been giving us so many ideas for the demonstration. I have fifteen pages of notes. I don't know what to do with all this information."

"Yeah, if we tried to talk about all that, we'd need a couple hours," Carrie said. "There's no way I want to talk for that long."

Kristy took the notebook and browsed through it. "You're right. There is a lot here. I don't know what to tell you. I think you two need to decide what would be the most convincing for the kids in the club."

# Chapter 8
# The Demonstration

"Good evening. This is Carrie Jackson for KZN-TV. We're at the site of what could be one of the most amazing discoveries in modern times. Archaeologist Rosalyn Marie has found what she claims is proof that horses evolved from small, doglike creatures. Rosalyn, are you ready to reveal your discovery to our television audience?"

"Thank you, Carrie. Yes, I'm certain this will remove any doubts people might have about the evolution of the horse." She nodded her head emphatically, trying her best to look adult and professional. "Yes, I'm sure it will."

"Okay, can you show it to us, then?"

"Why, yes, of course, it's right here in my hand." Rosalyn held up a closed fist.

"You have proof in your hand that horses evolved?"

Rosalyn nodded and slowly opened her hand, extending it toward Carrie.

"Um, what exactly is that?" Carrie motioned toward an imaginary cameraman. "You better move in a little closer so you can get this on camera. It's kind of small."

"It's a tooth!" Rosalyn beamed.

"A tooth? But, what does that prove?"

Rosalyn sighed and spoke slowly as if she were talking to a child. "This is a tooth used by a browsing animal such as Eohippus. It's very different from the tooth of a grazing animal that eats grass."

Carrie looked confused. "But—all you have is a tooth. I don't see how that proves anything."

"Honestly! Do I have to spell everything out for you? They discovered another animal in the layer of rock right above where I found this tooth." Rosalyn pointed off to her right. "It has one toe, like a horse. If that doesn't prove that the animal that had this tooth evolved into a horse-like creature, I don't know what will!"

Carrie looked off to the right, then back at the tooth in Rosalyn's hand and shrugged her shoulders. She raised her microphone. "Okay, folks, there you have it. Evolutionary proof from Rosalyn Marie! This is Carrie Jackson, signing off for KZN-TV."

Carrie and Rosie ran behind the table at the front of the room and turned to face the other 4-H members who were staring at them with puzzled expressions. *Well, at least we got their attention,* Rosie thought. She continued with the next part of their demonstration.

"At the last meeting you heard about a lot of animals people say lived millions of years ago—Eohippus, Orohippus, Merychippus, and some others. Evolutionists claim that those creatures are the great-great-great—I don't know how many great—grandparents of horses, like my Scamper. And that over the years they lost some toes, grew, then lost some ribs, and got a lot taller and more beautiful. What they don't tell you is that there is absolutely no evidence for any of their claims."

Rosie looked up and saw Emily scowling at her. She nodded to her sister, and Carrie picked up the presentation.

"Just like in the skit we acted out, archaeologists find bits of skeletons in different locations, sometimes on totally different continents, and claim they are connected. There's no place in the world that shows fossils in rock layers that match the pictures shown in books about horse evolution. In fact, some of the different animals have been found buried in the same layer of rock. If they evolved from one another over millions of years, how could two different kinds be found in the same layer?"

Rosie picked up a large piece of paper and handed it to Carrie who gave it to the girl at the beginning of the first row.

"You can pass that around. There was a big storm at our house the other day, and I saw my pencils blowing around over the top of that piece of paper. When the storm was over I looked and saw that picture of Scamper. It was amazing." Rosie paused and looked at the audience.

"Yeah, right. You expect us to believe that?" one of the kids said.

Rosie smiled. "If you don't believe that something as simple as a pencil sketch could happen by accident, how can you believe that things that are much more complicated—like people or horses, could evolve by chance?"

She waited a moment to let that sink in as the picture was being passed down the line. "When you look at that picture of Scamper, you know that someone drew it. When I look at the real Scamper, I know that Someone very intelligent created him. Carrie and I have spent the last two weeks learning about how specially the horse was designed from the bottom of his hooves to the tips of his ears."

Rosie held up her notebook. "I don't have time to go into all this, but I have fifteen pages of notes. We created a sheet that lists the information and made copies for each of you."

Carrie picked up a stack of papers and started them down the row.

"Evolution is not science," Rosie continued. "Science is knowledge gained by observing things and doing experiments. None of us were alive in the beginning to see what happened. It takes faith to believe in either evolution or creation." She picked her Bible up from the table. "The Bible says that God created the land animals on the sixth day of creation. That's what I believe. It makes a lot more sense than a little creature that looks like a badger turning into a horse or a fish growing wings and turning into a bird. That's not science. It's more like the fairy tale where the princess kisses a frog and it turns into a prince."

Carrie took the Bible from Rosie. "In the book of Job, God talks about the creation of the horse. He asked a man called Job, 'Hast thou given the horse strength? hast thou clothed his neck with thunder?' After many questions like that about creation, Job realized how little he knew about the world. There's nothing wrong with science. God gave us minds so we could discover ways to make our lives better. But as Rosie said, evolution is not science."

Carrie flipped ahead to the New Testament. "In Romans 1 verse 20 it says that we can clearly see God from the things that He made. When you leave here tonight, look around you. You'll see an amazing world where everything, from tiny seeds to huge elephants, shouts out that it was designed by God." Carrie closed the Bible and looked over at Rosie.

There was so much more Rosie wanted to say, but their demonstration had already gone on longer than most. Maybe she could talk to some of the kids after the meeting. "I guess that concludes our demonstration."

She and Carrie returned to their seats as the parents and members applauded. The club advisor stood up. "Thank you, girls. That was our last presentation, so I declare this meeting officially adjourned."

As everyone started toward the refreshment table, Emily and a friend stopped beside Rosie and Carrie. "If you two were trying to make me look stupid, I'd say it backfired. You didn't demonstrate anything except how dumb you are." Emily crumpled the information sheet the girls had handed out and tossed it in Rosie's lap. "You're not allowed to preach from the Bible at a 4-H meeting either. I'm going to report you."

Emily's friend laughed as she passed by. "You two look like the Bobbsey Twins in those T-shirts."

Carrie looked down at her shirt, then over at Rosie's. "Who are the Bobbsey Twins?"

Rosie shrugged and picked up the wad of paper, turning it over and over. "Were we that bad?"

"Actually I thought it went pretty well," Carrie said.

Kristy found her way over to the girls. "You two did a great job!"

"You're our mom. You have to say that." Rosie put both hands on her head and looked up at the ceiling. "We didn't get the farm. Our demonstration was a flop. What else can go wrong?"

"A couple of the moms already told me how much they appreciated it."

"That's nice, but I was hoping to convince the kids." Rosie could feel tears starting. She quickly wiped them away and looked around to see whether anyone had noticed. She didn't want the other kids to see her crying, especially Emily.

Katie, one of the youngest members of the club, approached them with a cookie in each hand. "Hi, Rosie. Hi, Carrie. I like your shirts."

"Thanks." Rosie managed a small smile.

"I learned all about evolution at school, but now I don't know what to believe."

Rosie sat up a little straighter. "There's a lot more I could tell you." She patted the chair beside her inviting Katie to have a seat, but the girl shook her head and ran over to sit beside her mother.

"See," Kristy said. "I bet you had a bigger impact than you think. Sometimes it's just about planting seeds. These kids will probably remember your demonstration for a long time. You never know, some day they may realize that you were right."

"Why can't they see it now?" Rosie asked. "How can they believe a frog formed out of slime in a swamp, but they can't believe God created everything? Creation makes so much more sense."

"It is hard to understand," Kristy said. "The Bible says that as Christians we can see with the eyes of our hearts. Some people think they have to have a scientific explanation for everything. No matter how ridiculous that 'science' may be, they would rather believe it than believe that an all-powerful God created everything."

The girls set the props from their demonstration on the kitchen table and went into Grandma's living room.

Rosie dropped glumly to the floor and was immediately greeted with slobbery puppy kisses. She curled up into a ball and laughed as she tried to push Tick away.

"How did the demonstration go?" Grandma asked.

"Emily was so nasty," Carrie said. "She said she was going to report us for using the Bible in our demonstration."

"I wouldn't worry about. . ."

Rosie sat up. "Grandma, your phone's ringing."

"Oh." Grandma looked around. "Where is it?"

Rosie followed the sound and located the cell phone buried inside the cushions of the recliner. She pushed the button and handed it to her grandmother.

"I'm sorry; he's not here right now. May I take a message?" Grandma motioned for Rosie to get her a pencil and a piece of paper. "All right, I'll have him call you."

"Do you know a Mark Miller?" Grandma jotted the name down on the paper Rosie handed her.

Kristy shook her head. "Never heard of him."

"He wanted to talk to Eric."

"Why would someone call for Eric on your cell phone?" Kristy asked.

"I don't know." Grandma shrugged. "Now, what were you saying about the demonstration?"

"They did a great job," Kristy said. "I should have recorded it for you."

"I have a better idea. The girls can do an encore performance just for me."

"Oh, Grandma." Rosie sighed and sprawled out on the floor. "Do we have to?"

Kristy held up her hand. "Hold on. I saw lights in the driveway. That must be Eric. He'll want to see the demonstration too."

Eric opened the front door. "Hey everyone! How did my little creation scientists do tonight?"

"Pretty good," Carrie said.

"You're just in time," Kristy said. "They were about to do the demonstration for Mom."

"Oh, Mark Miller called," Grandma said.

"Who?" Eric asked.

"Don't you know him? He called for you." Grandma held out the paper and her phone. "Here, the number's still on the phone."

"Why would someone call for me on your phone?"

"We were wondering the same thing," Grandma said.

Eric took the phone and hit dial. "Hello, yes this is. . . What? I'm sorry, I didn't hear you. Could you say that again?" He put his finger in his other ear and paced around the living room. "Yes, I was there. He what? Really?"

Rosie could hear the surprise in her father's voice. She jumped up and moved closer to him. "What, Dad? Who is it?"

Eric waved her away. "Yes, we sure do. We'll be there Monday. Thank you!" He pushed a button to end the call and stood staring at the phone.

"What is it, Eric?" Kristy looked concerned. "You look like you've seen a ghost or something."

"You're not going to believe this!" He dropped onto the couch.

"What?" they all said impatiently.

"Eric, tell us. What is it?" Kristy demanded.

A big smile spread across his face. "We got the farm!"

The bones in Rosie's legs suddenly felt as if they had been replaced with jello. She leaned over and put her hand on the back of the couch to steady herself. Her mouth opened, but no words came out.

"What are you talking about?" Grandma asked.

"The auction required a ten percent payment within a week of the sale, and the guy never came up with the money so it automatically goes to the second-highest bidder—which is us."

When Rosie had recovered from her initial shock, she let out a whoop and grabbed Carrie's hands. The girls danced and whirled around the living room.

"We need to meet at the bank Monday to make the down payment," Eric said.

Tears trickled down Grandma's cheeks. "I can't believe it! You were right all along, Rosie. It really was our farm."

Kristy looked at Grandma and Eric. "Should we call Julie? Or go over there and tell her? I don't want to give her a heart attack."

"Let me call her, Mom!" Rosie begged.

Kristy pulled out her phone and handed it to her.

"Hi. Aunt Julie! . . . Yes, we're fine. Guess what? . . . We're going to be your new neighbors!"

Rosie laughed. "No, I'm not crazy. We got the farm!" She listened for a moment, then handed the phone to Grandma. "You talk to her. She keeps saying I'm crazy."

Grandma took the phone. "Yes, it's true." She explained everything, nodding her head repeatedly as if Julie could see her through the phone.

"Can we take the horses over tomorrow?" Rosie asked.

Kristy laughed. "No, I imagine it will take a few weeks to get all the paperwork settled."

# Chapter 9

# Horse Thief

Rosie leaned out Scamper's stall door and watched her grandmother limp down the barn aisle. "Grandma, I can't get used to seeing you with your cast off. It seems like you had it on forever."

"No kidding. My leg feels all shriveled up, but I'm glad to be walking again without crutches."

Grandma rubbed Kezzie's forehead. "You're getting better every day too, aren't you, girl?" Grandma slipped the horse's halter on.

Carrie led Zach out of his stall. "Sassy will be happy to see her old friends again—especially Kezzie."

Grandma looked over toward Scamper's stall. "Are you ready, Rosie?"

"Almost." Rosie finished braiding a bright red ribbon in Scamper's mane and led him out into the aisle. He tossed his head and looked at the other horses as if he were showing off a bit.

"Well, isn't he handsome!" Grandma said.

"He wanted to look special for the trip to his new home. He's never lived anywhere else but here." Rosie felt a twinge of nervousness. As excited as she was to finally be moving to the new farm, it was still hard to leave this place. She breathed in deeply as if memorizing the scents of leather, hay, and horses that were Sonrise Stable. There were so many memories here—learning to ride on Jet, raising and training Scamper, meeting Carrie in this barn, Cousins Camp, even the possum scare during their almost-campout. Jemimah rubbed up against her leg. Rosie reached down and petted the calico barn cat. "Don't worry. We wouldn't leave you or Katy."

Grandma started out of the barn with Kezzie. "Let's load the horses; then we'll get the cats."

Soon they had all three horses in the trailer and the two barn cats in a crate in the back of the truck.

"Aw, they're meowing like crazy," Carrie said. "They look scared."

"They don't understand what's happening." Grandma scratched Katy's head through the wire crate. "Let me run over and get June Bug, then we'll be ready to go."

Rosie laughed. "I want to see you run, Grandma."

"Okay, walk. You know what I mean." Grandma headed toward the house.

Rosie and Carrie sat on the tailgate of the truck swinging their legs. Soon Rosie grew impatient and hopped down. "What's taking Grandma so long? I can't wait until we get the horses to the new farm."

Finally Grandma opened the gate and walked down the path with a cat carrier. When she reached the truck, she shoved the carrier between the crate that held the other cats and the side of the truck bed. June Bug hissed and growled at her neighbors, Katy and Jemimah.

Rosie pointed to a line of blood dripping down her grandmother's hand. "What happened?"

Grandma held up her hand and stared at it. "June Bug had a change of heart. She decided she wanted to stay here."

Carrie ran to get the first aid kit from the truck and pulled out a box of Band-Aids. She fished one out and handed it to her grandmother.

Grandma ripped the wrapper open and stuck the Band-Aid across her hand. "After she scratched me, I dropped her. Then I couldn't catch her, so I had to throw a blanket over her to wrestle her into the carrier. Maybe I should have left her here, but I figured she'd scare people away from buying this place."

Grandma looked over everything in the back of the truck. "I guess that's it. We better leave. Your dad will be wondering what happened to us."

"It's my turn to sit in front!" Carrie ran around and jumped into the front seat. Grandma and Rosie climbed in the other side.

During the hour-long drive the girls kept turning to check on the horses in the trailer and the cats in the back of the truck. Rosie was so excited she felt like a firecracker on the Fourth of July—ready to explode at any moment. Although she spent a lot of time at her grandmother's farm, she had always lived in a small house in a crowded subdivision. She couldn't believe she and Carrie were going to have their own riding stable.

Finally they reached the point where the road turned to gravel and Grandma slowed down. Carrie pointed up ahead. "There's Grandma's house!"

Rosie leaned forward so she could see out the front window. "Hey, I'm supposed to say that."

Eric had dug up the Sonrise Stable sign with its horse and cross, and moved it to the entrance of the new farm. The place was already beginning to shape up—the grass had been mowed and a shiny, silver mailbox sat on the post across the road from the driveway. Grandma drove slowly down the drive and stopped in front of the barn.

Eric came out of the house to meet them. "Julie brought Sassy and her kids' horses over a few hours ago. Sassy's anxious to see her old friends."

Rosie backed Scamper out of the trailer. He arched his neck, ears pricked forward, and looked all around. "This is your new home, Scamp. Do you like it?" The pony whinnied shrilly, announcing his arrival. Answering whinnies and a loud bray came from inside the barn.

Carrie patted Scamper's neck. "Why does he sound like such a girl?"

"I don't know," Rose laughed. "Maybe he needs some voice lessons." She led Scamper in circles around the driveway while she waited for the others to unload.

Grandma backed Kezzie out next. "Did you hear your old friend, Sassy?" The mare's eyes grew wide as if she were thinking *Oh, no! I thought I got rid of that annoying animal.*

When Carrie had unloaded Zach, they led the horses into the stable.

"Here you go, boy. This is your stall. See, it has your name on it." Carrie pointed to the nameplate Rosie had made for Zach that was attached to the front of his stall.

Sassy pranced back and forth in her stall. Patches, Jessie's horse, was her neighbor on the left and Kezzie was on her right. She brayed a friendly greeting to Kezzie and tried to sniff noses with her. Kezzie squealed and stomped her foot.

"They say absence makes the heart grow fonder," Grandma said, "but I don't think that's the case with Kezzie. She certainly doesn't like that mule. We may need to rearrange horses so she's not right beside Sassy."

The girls ran back to the truck to unload their saddles and the rest of their tack. They set everything up in the stall across from Scamper.

Eric looked at the collection of cats in the back of the truck. "What do you want done with these guys?"

Grandma grabbed one end of Jemimah and Katy's crate. "Can you help me with these two? I'll leave them in the crate in one of the stalls for a day or so until they start to feel like this is home. I don't want them to run away."

Eric helped carry the crate into the barn and returned to the truck. He peeked into the front of the cat carrier and jumped back when its occupant slammed against the carrier door, spitting and growling. "Uh, let me guess. You have June Bug in there."

Grandma laughed. "I'll let her out in a minute. I don't think she'll run off."

"We can always hope," Eric laughed. He turned to the girls and grew serious. "We have a lot of work to do if we're going to have this house ready to live in before bad weather arrives. Jonathan and I will be working as much as we can, but we'll need everyone's help."

Carrie and Rosie nodded.

"You'll be staying in the apartment with Grandma until we're finished with the house. That will mean less running around for your mom and me. We're trusting you to get some studying done without being told. You'll have time to ride when you're not needed at the house."

"Okay, Dad." Rosie looked around. "Where's a hammer? Do you want me to start fixing up the house?"

Eric laughed. "No. Not yet. I'm going into town to buy some lumber. Why don't you two explore until I get back. Don't ride yet. The horses need a chance to get accustomed to their new surroundings before you get on them."

Grandma pulled grocery bags from the back seat of the truck. "At least I can feed everyone now. I'll see what I can whip up for dinner tonight in my cute little kitchen."

"Sounds good! I'll be back in a few hours."

The girls helped their grandmother carry the remaining supplies inside. Eric had purchased a trundle bunk bed to make the most use of the space in the small apartment. Rosie claimed the top bunk and Grandma the bottom. That left Carrie with the trundle bed that pulled out from below Grandma's. It would be kept pushed underneath except at night.

"Do you need anything else, Grandma?" Carrie asked.

"No, I'll putter around in here, getting organized. I'd love to go with you, but I don't think my leg is ready for. . ."

The girls were gone even before Grandma finished her thought. They ran across the arena to the other side of the barn. Rosie stepped into the first stall and patted the wall. "I can't wait until Dad turns this into a bunkhouse for the campers."

"For the girls you mean," Carrie said.

"Yeah, Dad will have to put the boys somewhere else," Rosie said. "If there are any. Boys are so weird. Not many of them like horses."

"Jared does. And Billy King."

Rosie scowled. "Don't remind me of him! Come on. I'll race you to the woods."

The girls ran across the pasture and into the woods. "Let's go around the outside," Rosie suggested. "We should make a circle trail that goes around the outer edge of the woods, then we can have branches that come off of it and cross through the middle."

Carrie looked around. "We won't get lost will we?"

"Nah." Rosie tapped the side of her head. "I have a compass inside my brain. I'm really good at directions."

The girls tramped around the property. Although their dad and uncle had mowed the pastures, the woods were still a little on the wild side. The girls pushed through the saplings and brush and walked along downed trees as if they were gymnasts on a balance beam.

They approached a clearing, and Carrie pointed to a huge oak tree. "Isn't that the tree Jared wants to build the tree house in?"

Rosie looked up and nodded. "Yeah. He tied a rope around one of the branches to mark it. We should make a trail that comes right up to the tree house."

"If we're going to lead rides for the campers, we'll have to have all the trails memorized," Carrie said.

"Yeah, but some of them will be secret, that only the family will know about," Rosie said.

The girls wandered around the woods, climbing up and down the ravines, and crossing the shallow creek on stones that peeked up out of the water.

Rosie sat down on the bank and tossed a few pebbles into the sparkling clear water. "This is going to be so much fun. I can't believe we're going to have our own horse camps."

"We should have bonfires out here and roast hot dogs and marshmallows."

"Mmm. You're making me hungry." Rosie stood up and dusted off her jeans. "Let's go back and see if Grandma has dinner ready."

They looked around. Most of the trees had lost their leaves. There were so many of them that no matter which way they turned, everything looked the same—row after row of tall, gray trunks.

"Which way?" Carrie asked.

"Which way do you think?" Rosie asked.

Carrie pointed to her left.

"I was thinking right." Rosie started off in that direction. Carrie looked back to the left, then reluctantly turned and followed her sister.

After the girls had walked another twenty minutes, Carrie stopped. "Hey, Compass Brain. We're back at the tree house tree. We went in a big circle."

"No we didn't!"

Carrie pointed to a branch over their head. Rosie looked up and saw the rope Jared had tied to the tree. "Oh, I guess we did."

Carrie turned to her left. "I knew we should have gone this way."

Rosie followed. "Yeah. I knew that too. I was just testing you to see whether you'd be a good trail guide or not."

Carrie laughed. "Yeah, right."

The girls finally saw an opening in the trees and the pasture up ahead. Rosie spotted her dad's truck at the house. "Dad's back."

As they came closer, Carrie pointed to a rusty, red pickup parked near the barn. "Who is that?"

"I don't know. Shhh!" Rosie whispered. She crept around the corner of the stable with Carrie close behind. When she reached the front door she stopped, pressing herself up against the wall. She held her finger to her lips to keep Carrie quiet and peeked around the barn door. She jerked her head back. "Oh no!" Rosie turned pale. "He's here."

"Who's here?" Carrie tried to move past Rosie, so she could see around the door, but Rosie held her arm out to stop her.

"He's right by Zach's stall. I told you he would try to steal him!"

"Someone's trying to steal my horse? Who?"

"Shh! It's Billy," Rosie whispered. "Come on. We need to tell Dad!" She whirled around, crouched down, and ran in a wide arc toward the house so Billy King wouldn't see her. Carrie followed. When they arrived at the house, Rosie pounded on the back door and yelled, "Dad, call the police! Hurry!"

The door flew open, and Eric rushed outside. "What? What happened?" He quickly scanned the girls to see whether they were injured.

"Call the police," Rosie repeated breathlessly.

"Rosie, what's wrong? Is it Grandma? Did something happen to her?" Eric started running toward the barn.

"No! Don't go out there. He's there!"

Eric slid to a stop on the loose gravel and turned around. "Rosie, you're not making any sense. Who's out there? Carrie, what is she talking about?"

"Billy's trying to steal my horse!"

"Oh." Eric heaved a sigh of relief. "You two scared me half to death."

"Aren't you going to call the police?" Rosie persisted.

"No, Rosie. He asked me if he could go see Zach."

"What?"

"I ran into him in town and offered him a job. He's going to help us fix up the house."

Rosie stared at her father. "You're kidding."

"No, I'm not. He's supposed to be a very good carpenter. We can use the help if we hope to get the house finished by Thanksgiving. He's out of school now and doesn't have a job so it will help him out too."

Rosie clenched her teeth. She didn't understand why her dad was interested in helping Billy out. "Come on." She pulled Carrie's arm. "Let's go lock Zach's stall." They started toward the barn and met Billy halfway as he returned to the house. He smiled at the girls and opened his mouth to speak, but Rosie glared at him and walked by without saying a word.

# Chapter 10

# Grandma Rides Again

Billy pounded the last nail into a wooden brace he was building and raised it to an upright position. "Jared, can you help me with this?"

Jared and the girls had been removing trash from the house and throwing it into a dumpster. He ran over to Billy. "What do you need?"

"Hold this while I hammer it into place. You girls better stand back," Billy warned. Rosie scowled, but she and the other girls moved away from the porch.

Jared held the brace as Billy positioned it under the sagging porch roof and pounded the bottom with his hammer. The roof gradually began to rise to a normal height. Billy climbed on the ladder and nailed a two by six across the porch roof for support.

Jared looked up at him. "You're really good at this."

"I know a little about it." Billy smiled. "I helped my dad build our barn a few years ago."

"I'm going to build a tree house in the woods," Jared said.

"Cool." Billy turned himself nearly upside down on the ladder so he could hammer a few nails in the underside of the roof. "I can give you a hand if you want."

"Sure!" Jared said.

"Traitor," Rosie whispered under her breath. She gave Jared a withering look, but he didn't seem to notice. She motioned for the girls to follow her back into the house.

Inside, Eric and Jonathan were rewiring electrical outlets while Grandma, Kristy, and Julie stripped wallpaper. Eric looked up when the girls came in. "How's Billy coming with the porch? The way he's been working we're going to have this place finished sooner than I thought."

"Is that all anyone can talk about anymore—how great Billy is?" Rosie griped.

Eric frowned. "Rosie, we need to have a talk later about your attitude."

Rosie said nothing in reply. She dropped her bucket on the floor and began throwing wallpaper scraps and other trash into it. Had everyone forgotten about Billy abusing his horse, Bandit, at the fair last summer? Since her dad had bought Bandit to rescue him from Billy, she assumed he would be on her side. When the bucket was full, Rosie lugged it out the front door.

"My dad taught me how to do most of this stuff," Billy was explaining to Jared.

Rosie dropped her bucket down on the porch and looked up at him. "Did your mom ever teach you how to be kind to animals?"

Billy threw his hammer down. It hit the wooden floor of the porch and bounced off into the grass. "No, as a matter of fact she didn't!"

Rosie jumped back, a little frightened by his reaction. As he turned to face her, she could see that his face had turned dark red.

"Come on." Carrie tugged on Rosie's jacket sleeve. "Just pretend he's not here."

Rosie picked up her bucket and headed for the dumpster. She climbed the stepladder, turned the bucket upside down and banged it against the side, smashing her finger between the bucket and the dumpster wall. "Ow!" The sudden pain caused her to release her grip and the bucket fell inside. Tears stung her eyes. She shook her hand back and forth and glanced toward the boys to see whether they had noticed.

Billy smiled and waved at her.

*Oh! He makes me so mad!* There was nothing Rosie could do now but climb into the dumpster to retrieve the bucket. She pulled herself up, flipped her legs over the side and dropped down on top of the trash. *Eww, it stinks in here.* Holding her nose, she grabbed the bucket and tossed it over the side wall. She climbed out, not even looking in Billy's direction.

"Rosie, why don't you come with me?" Eric said after the family had finished eating supper that night in the little apartment in the barn.

Rosie's heart sank. *Oh, no. I'm in trouble now.* She followed her father out to his truck.

Eric opened the passenger door and Rosie climbed in, leaning back against the worn leather seat. She looked straight ahead at the stable. Her dad sat in the driver's seat and smiled at her. "There's not much of a chance for privacy around here, so I thought this was as good a place as any for a little talk."

Rosie smiled weakly.

"Thanks for all your help with the house. I appreciate it. Are you beginning to understand what I said about houses always falling apart? Not magically fixing themselves?"

Rosie nodded. She had gone to bed exhausted every night that week after working long hours each day on the house. Were they ever going to have the fun she had looked forward to when they first talked about buying the farm? But she knew they weren't here to talk about the house. She waited for her dad to get around to the topic she suspected he had in mind—Billy King.

"I've been thinking a lot about creation since you and Carrie started working on that demonstration. You believe that God created each of us, right?"

Rosie nodded again.

"And that He wants each of us to be saved? Remember how much we all prayed for Carrie and how happy we were when she became a Christian?"

"I prayed for her a lot!" Rosie smiled. Maybe her dad had forgotten all about Billy.

"It says in the Bible that when we become Christians, the old passes away and we become new creations."

Rosie's neck was getting stiff from turning to look at her dad. She shifted sideways in the seat so she faced him. "Yeah, Carrie has changed. She's not nearly as shy as she used to be."

"What about Billy? Do you think he could change too?"

Rosie's smile vanished. How had her dad managed to sneak that in?

"Would you pray for Billy like you did for Carrie?"

Rosie crossed her arms and frowned. "But Dad, he was so mean to Zach, and he made me lose my class at the fair. Scamper and I would have a trophy and blue ribbon if it weren't for Billy's cheating."

Eric nodded. "This is no excuse for his behavior, but he hasn't had the same kind of life you've had."

"What do you mean?"

"You've been raised in a Christian family and homeschooled. You've been in church every week from the time you were a few days old."

Rosie nodded. She loved church. She couldn't remember ever missing a week.

"But that doesn't make you better than someone that hasn't had those advantages. In fact the Bible says that when God gives someone more, He expects more from them."

Rosie picked at a spot on her jeans. *Does Dad think I'm stuck up?*

"Did you know Billy's mom died when he was two? I doubt if he remembers her at all."

*Didn't your mom teach you. . .* The question she had asked Billy earlier that day popped into her head. She swallowed the lump that was rising in her throat and shook her head. No wonder Billy had been so angry at her.

"His dad has raised him by himself. He works a lot, so he's not always there for Billy."

Rosie tried to imagine what life would be like without her mom. The thought was so awful she pushed it out of her mind. "But why does he have to be so mean?"

"I don't know. Winning horse shows probably made him feel important, like he was worth something, so he did whatever it took to make sure he won."

Rosie struggled with her feelings. Knowing Billy didn't have a mother made her a little more sympathetic toward him, but she was still angry about the things he had done.

"God is in the business of turning people's lives around. Sometimes the worst sinners can become the most on fire for God. Remember Paul? He started out persecuting Christians and having them killed, but later became one of the strongest believers and wrote most of the New Testament."

"I guess Carrie and I can start praying for Billy," Rosie said grudgingly, "but I still don't like him very much."

Eric smiled. "I believe God will soften your heart toward Billy. It's hard to pray for someone and continue to dislike him."

Rosie thought she might be able to pray for Billy, but she couldn't imagine ever liking him. She closed her eyes and sighed. When she opened them again, the dilapidated house caught her attention. It made her tired just looking at it. "When are we going to move in, Dad? I'm tired of working all the time."

"You and me both." Eric patted her leg. "Run and get your mom. She and I will head back to our old house so she can get to an appointment in the morning. I know everyone's tired, but if we keep working, before long our lives will get back to normal."

Rosie leaned over and hugged her father. "I love you, Dad."

"I love you, too, Rosie."

The next day they all decided they could use a break. Everyone quit work early and gathered in the riding arena for Grandma's first ride since the trail riding accident. Kezzie had almost fully recovered, but Grandma wanted to let her rest a few more months before riding her. Today she would be taking her first mule ride.

Billy stood alone, watching from over the arena gate on the opposite side of the barn. Julie led Sassy up to Grandma. The mule kept turning to look back toward the aisle where the other horses were.

"Hold still, Mule Head," Rosie called out. "Grandma's going to ride you."

Grandma approached the mule cautiously and looked at Julie. "Are you sure she's ready for this?"

"She's ready if you are," Julie replied. "I don't think she has a mean bone in her body. She's just spoiled. Don't expect her to respond to a light touch like Kezzie does—she hasn't picked things up as quickly as I had hoped."

Jonathan carried a mounting block over and set it beside the mule.

"Thanks. I'll need that. She's taller than Kezzie." Grandma stepped onto the mounting block, put her left foot in the stirrup and swung her right leg over the mule's back. She smiled and leaned down to pet Sassy. "Would you look at those ears! They look even bigger from up here."

Julie handed her the reins and Grandma urged Sassy forward. They made a trip around the arena; then Sassy stopped by the gate closest to her stall. She put her head over it and brayed, but the horses ignored her.

"Poor Sassy. She never seems to realize that none of the horses like her," Julie said. "She keeps trying to make friends with them. It's rather pathetic."

Grandma squeezed her legs and signaled Sassy to move forward, but she refused to budge.

"Make her go, Grandma," Jessie shouted. "Do you need my mom to give you riding lessons?"

"Yes, it looks like I might need some mule riding lessons," Grandma laughed. She used her legs more strongly, but Sassy just turned her head around and stared at her. Shaking her head and laughing, Julie took the reins and led the mule back to the center of the arena.

"Guess I'll keep her away from that gate for now."
Grandma asked Sassy for a little more speed, and she picked
up a slow, smooth jog. She waved at the girls as she passed.
"It feels good to be back in the saddle." Grandma jogged
Sassy in circles at the far end of the arena. She slowed her
back to a walk and made another lap around the ring. When
Sassy spotted Billy standing by the other gate, she stopped and
nudged his arm. Billy reached through the gate and started to
scratch the mule's ears.

"No! Don't do that!"

Billy jerked his hand back. "I—I'm sorry…"

"It's all right, Billy. I was kidding," Grandma said. "She loves to have her ears scratched so much I figured I'd never get her to move again." Grandma smiled as Billy reached through the gate to scratch Sassy. The mule tipped her head sideways and got a goofy look in her eyes.

"Why don't you take her for a spin?" Grandma offered.

"Oh, no." Billy waved his hands. "This is your day to ride."

"This is plenty for me. My leg is still weak. I'll get back into it gradually." Grandma slid down and held out the reins.

Billy walked through the gate and closed it. "I've never ridden a mule before."

"I hadn't either," Grandma laughed. "You couldn't do any worse than I did."

Billy threw the right rein up over Sassy's neck and walked to her left side.

"Billy"

He turned to look at Grandma.

"I hope you've changed your ways. I'm trusting you with my mule."

"Yes, ma'am. I'll treat her right."

"You better," Grandma warned. "Mules don't forget, and they know how to get even."

Billy nodded and swung easily into the saddle. "Wow, she does have huge ears." Soon he had her jogging around the arena. "Does she canter?" he asked Julie as they passed by.

"Once in a blue moon," Julie laughed.

Billy signaled for a canter, and Sassy responded immediately on the correct lead. Julie stared in amazement. "How'd you do that? I've been working with her for weeks, and I still have a hard time getting her to canter."

Billy shrugged and smiled.

"Oh, great." Rosie frowned. "Not only is Billy the world's greatest carpenter, now he's a mule whisperer too."

"He's doing really well with her," Carrie said. "You haven't been able to get her to canter either."

"Yes, I have!"

"Yeah, for about two steps," Carrie laughed.

Rosie glared at Carrie. "Whose side are you on, anyway? It was your horse he was whipping at the fair or have you forgotten that already?"

"I haven't forgotten, but he seems like he's changed since he's been working here."

"All I know is I wouldn't trust him for a minute with Scamper." Rosie turned her attention back to Billy and Sassy.

Billy slowed the mule to a walk, made a few more trips around the arena, then dismounted and handed the reins to Julie.

"You seem to have a knack with her. If you have time when you're done working, you're welcome to ride her," Julie said.

"You mean it?" Billy smiled. "That would be great."

"Would you like to stay and have supper with us tonight, Billy?" Grandma asked.

"Oh, no," Billy shook his head. "I better be getting home. Thanks for letting me ride." He turned and hurried toward his truck.

Rosie heaved a sigh of relief. It was bad enough working on the house all day around Billy. The last thing she wanted was to have him sitting across the dinner table from her.

# Chapter 11

# Ride 'Em Cowboy

Billy and Jared stepped out the back door of the house and watched Rosie as she tried to pound a nail into a piece of scrap wood. She hit the board more often than the nail.

"You hammer like a girl," Billy laughed. "Do you want me to show you the right way to do it?"

"No thank you," Rosie snapped. "I'm doing fine by myself."

"Yeah, I can see that," Billy said. "What are you trying to make anyway?"

Rosie hesitated, but Jessie piped up. "We're making a dog house for Tick!"

Billy and Jared looked at the hodgepodge of boards nailed together and burst into laughter. They headed toward Billy's truck for more paint.

Rosie glared at Jessie. "Why'd you have to tell them that?"

Jessie shrugged. "I thought that's what we were making."

Carrie sat on the sidewalk with the pup stretched out beside her. "It's okay. Tick doesn't need a doghouse anyway. She likes to sleep with me at night."

"Only because I'm on the top bunk," Rosie insisted.

The boys stopped again on their way back inside. "Do you girls want to ride with us this afternoon?" Jared asked. "Billy and I are going to finish marking the outer trail."

"Yeah!" the twins said excitedly.

Rosie scowled. She felt as if she had lost a cousin. All Jared did anymore was hang around Billy. It seemed like Jared couldn't even think for himself now. It was always, "Billy said this" or "Billy did that." The boys worked together all day and rode horses almost every evening.

"I guess so," Rosie said.

"Good. We're almost finished painting the first coat downstairs," Jared said. "While it's drying, we're going to ride."

Rosie and Carrie finished saddling Scamper and Zach and helped the twins with their horses. They started for the arena, but Rosie changed her mind and headed for the door. "Let's go check the mail."

They led the horses outside. Everyone mounted and they started down the long driveway.

"When are you guys going to move in?" Jessie asked as she rode alongside Rosie. "I'm tired of working on your house every day."

"I'm going to tell Mom," Jamie said. "That's not very polite."

"It's okay," Rosie said. "I'm tired of working on it too, and I live here."

"All that's left now is painting and putting carpet in the bedrooms," Carrie said.

"Dad says we're moving in next week—just in time for Thanksgiving," Rosie said.

"I'll be thankful for that." Jessie urged Patches into a trot.

Jamie shook her head at her sister. "Don't pay any attention to her. It's fun having you guys so close. I love being able to come over here on my bike and ride horses with you and Carrie."

They all stopped when they reached the gravel road. Rosie checked both directions for cars.

"Don't worry," Jessie said. "No one ever comes down this road."

Rosie guided Scamper over to the mailbox. "Whoa, boy." She stopped in front of it and used leg pressure to move him sideways so she could reach the mailbox door. She pulled out a stack of mail and looked through it. "Hey, I got a letter!"

Carrie rode over. "Who's it from?"

Rosie shrugged. "I don't know."

"Did I get a letter from Lauren?"

"I don't know that either. Here." Rosie handed Carrie the rest of the mail and ripped open her envelope. She read the brief note silently and smiled.

"What is it?" Jessie asked. "A letter from your boyfriend?"

Rosie scowled at her. "Of course not. It's from Katie, a girl in our 4-H club."

"What does she want?" Carrie asked.

"Mom told her about our summer camp, and she wants to come."

"Yay! Our first camper." Jamie cheered.

"Why would she come to our camp?" Carrie asked. "Doesn't she have her own horse?"

Rosie shook her head. "No, she was taking the Horseless Horse project. She wants to know if I'm going to have an art class during the camp, and she wants to buy one of the creation T-shirts we made."

"An art class would be fun," Carrie said. "Hey, maybe we can start our own T-shirt business too!"

Jared and Billy rode up on Scout and Sassy. "We looked all over for you girls! What are you doing out here yakking? I thought you were going to ride with us."

"We got tired of waiting on you slowpokes, so we came out to get the mail." Rosie stuck the letter in her jacket pocket. "We'll drop the mail off at the house and meet you at the barn." She signaled Scamper to canter, and the other girls followed her across the front yard.

When they met back at the barn, Jared was attaching a saddlebag to the back of his saddle. He stuck two cans of white spray paint in the pocket. Billy added cans of red paint to Sassy's saddlebag.

"What's the paint for?" Jessie asked.

"It's for the trail markers." Jared mounted Scout.

"But why do you need two colors?" Jessie asked.

"How many times do I have to explain it to you?" Jared sighed. "White on the right. If you turn right from the barn and go counter clockwise around the trail, you'll see the white markings on the trees on the right side. If you go left, clockwise, you'll see the red marks on the left."

"Okay," Jessie said. "You don't have to be so crabby about it." She rode Patches over beside Rosie and Carrie.

The group rode single file across the back pasture and entered the woods. The trail was rough, with thick brush and saplings covering the planned route. They hadn't ridden far when they came to a large log across the trail.

Billy stopped and looked around at the tangle of undergrowth in the woods. "It's going to take us a long time to clear all this."

Rosie frowned. The idea that Billy might continue working at the farm after the house was finished had never occurred to her. She had assumed that once they moved in she wouldn't see him again. "I think Dad and Uncle Jonathan are going to clear the trail themselves."

A strange look flickered across Billy's face. "Uh, yeah, that's what I meant. Come on, Sassy." He urged the mule forward. She hunkered down, then jumped cleanly over the log. Billy turned in the saddle, with a big smile. "Let's see if your fat, little pony can do that."

Rosie looked at the log, then down at Scamper. "He can do anything old Mule Head can do, only better. And he's not fat!" She squeezed her legs, signaling him to go forward. Confused, he moved sideways, then started backing up. Billy laughed.

Rosie could feel her face growing hot. She turned her horse around and steered him toward the log again. Scamper placed one foot on it, then the other and stood perched with both front legs on top of the log, looking quite pleased with himself.

Carrie laughed. "That's how he looked that time he stood in the wheelbarrow."

"Mmm-huh, great jump, Rosie," Billy laughed.

Rosie pulled back on the reins and Scamper stepped down from the log. She urged him forward again, and he stepped over it, the log nearly touching his stomach.

"He could jump it if he wanted to," Rosie insisted. "It's probably just too small for him."

Billy smiled and continued down the trail. They stopped periodically while Jared marked one side of a tree and Billy marked the other. When they reached the far end of the property, they started around the loop that would take them back to the stable.

Jessie pulled back on Patches. "Stop, guys. I hear something!"

When the noise of the horses tromping through the brush and dry leaves died down, they all listened. The strange wailing sound seemed to echo off the trees, making it difficult to tell what it was or where it was coming from.

"It's a cat," Rosie said.

"No." Jared shook his head. "It's a bird. There aren't any cats out here."

Carrie stood up in her stirrups and looked around. She suddenly looked very serious. "Maybe it's a bird evolving into a cat."

"Good one, Carrie," Jessie said.

They all laughed—except Billy. "What's wrong with that?" he said. "It could happen."

Rosie stared at him. Did he actually believe that? Or was he just trying to annoy her? She remembered the talk she'd had with her father and decided it wasn't worth arguing with Billy right now. She and Carrie could ask him about it later. "Be quiet guys, so I can hear."

They all held the horses still and looked around.

"Over there!" Rosie pointed. "It *is* a cat!"

An orange and white kitten peeked out from a hollow log. "Here, Carrie, hold my reins." Rosie jumped off Scamper. The sudden movement frightened the kitten, and it ran back inside the log.

Rosie walked over and sat on top of the log. She picked up a twig and moved it from side to side in the leaves. The curious kitten swiveled his head back and forth following the movement of the twig. Rosie gradually pushed the stick out a little farther. When the kitten pounced on it, she dropped the stick and wrapped both hands around him.

"Gotcha." She picked it up and scratched the kitten's head. "You didn't evolve, did you? I wonder what happened to your mother." Rosie turned to the others. "I told you it was a cat."

"Great." Billy frowned. "What are you going to do with it now?"

"Take him home, of course."

"You don't want to walk all the way back. Here, put him in my saddlebag," Billy offered.

"I don't need your help." Rosie started back toward Scamper. "Carrie can you hold him for a minute?"

Carrie dismounted and traded Scamper's reins for the kitten. "What are you doing?"

Rosie got back on Scamper and held her hands out. "Hand him up to me."

Carrie looked doubtful. "Are you sure? I don't think cats like to ride horses."

"Rosie, that's not a good idea," Billy said. "He'll probably scratch Scamper, and then you'll both get dumped."

Rosie ignored Billy and took the kitten out of Carrie's hands. She unzipped her jacket, tucked him inside, and zipped it up partway.

The kitten poked his front paws out. All anyone could see
were his paws and his head. Dark orange stripes ran back
from each side of his face and the top of his head. He looked

over the scene with his greenish-gray eyes and rested his chin on his paws, settling in for the ride.

Rosie squeezed her legs, and Scamper started off. As they walked through the woods, Rosie looked down and watched the kitten's eyes blink. She could tell he wanted to stay awake, but the rhythmic motion of Scamper's gait was rocking him to sleep. "See, I told you he'd be fine."

When they neared the edge of the woods, Scamper realized they were heading back to the stable and dinner. He picked up his pace, walking so fast that he began bumping into the back of Sassy.

"Stay back, Rosie. You know how mules kick," Billy warned.

"I'm trying," Rosie said. She kept one hand around the bulge in her jacket, holding the kitten in place and with the other she pulled the reins to slow Scamper down, but it wasn't enough.

Sassy's big ears went flat back on her neck. She squealed loudly and lashed out with both hind feet.

Scamper jumped straight up in the air and turned sideways to avoid Sassy's sharp heels. Rosie felt herself sliding off and grabbed for the saddle horn. She pulled herself back upright in the saddle and managed to stop Scamper.

"Whoa, Sassy." Billy turned the mule around to face Rosie. "Are you okay?"

"Yeah, I'm all right." She looked down at the kitten. He opened his eyes and yawned. Rosie laughed. "I guess he's fine too."

"Woohoo! Ride 'em cowboy!" Jessie yelled.

"Hey," Rosie said. "That's a great name for him—Cowboy."

Carrie laughed. "We must have the only cat in the world that likes to ride horses."

"I hope June Bug doesn't eat him for supper," Billy said.

"That's awful, Billy." Rosie squeezed the kitten close to her. "Why don't you keep that mule under control anyway?"

"I was kidding, Rosie. And this mule is fine as long as you keep your stupid pony off her rear end." He paused a minute, then looked at her. "Are you going to stay mad at me forever? Couldn't we call a truce or something?"

There was an awkward silence as everyone turned to look at Rosie.

Rosie scratched Cowboy's head. "I'll think about it." She signaled Scamper to walk. "An apology would be nice," she said, but she wasn't sure Billy heard her.

# Chapter 12

# Thanksgiving

After they unsaddled and fed the horses, Billy and Jared walked back toward the house to resume painting. Eric met them partway. He held out a check to Billy. "This should cover the last of the work you've done."

Billy stuffed the check into the pocket of his jeans. "I thought I was going to help you finish up."

Eric shook his head. "That's okay. We can finish the painting ourselves, then we'll be ready to move in."

Billy nodded. He turned, shoulders slumping and started toward his truck.

"Wait a second, Billy. I wanted to invite you to join us for Thanksgiving."

Billy paused, but didn't quite turn all the way around. "Oh, no. I couldn't do that. My dad and I will do something together."

"No, I insist," Eric said. "We want you to come. Bring your dad too. Without you it would have been New Years before we finished. You'll come. Won't you?"

"He'll come." Jared punched Billy's arm. "Right?"

Billy smiled and started toward his truck. "I'll see what my dad says."

On Saturday morning a caravan of friends drove pickups down the long drive to the house. The cousins helped carry what seemed to be a never-ending stream of cardboard boxes into the house, each marked with the name of the room where it belonged.

Hours later, as Rosie helped unload the last truck, she picked up a large box and turned it around to see where she needed to take it. "Trophy room." Grandma had saved some of the trophies and ribbons Rosie's mother and aunts had won at horse shows when they were younger. A small room in the new house would be used to display the awards, along with framed photographs of family members and their horses.

Rosie swallowed a lump of disappointment. She didn't have a trophy or even a ribbon to add to the collection. Even Carrie, who hadn't been riding nearly as long, already had both. *If it weren't for Billy, Scamper and I would have won that class at the fair.* Rosie shook her head trying to get rid of the negative thoughts. She set the box down in the trophy room and hurried to her bedroom. Carrie was sitting on the floor in the middle of the room watching their dad assemble a bed.

"Why don't you help me unpack my stuff?" Rosie said. "Then I'll help you unpack yours."

"Okay." Carrie opened a box of books and arranged them on Rosie's bookcase. "I'm going to kind of miss staying in the barn with you and Grandma."

"Me too," Rosie agreed. "It was fun being so close to the horses. Hey, Dad, what are we going to do with the apartment now?"

Eric finished tightening a bolt in the bed frame. "I was thinking about asking. . ."

Just then Grandma entered the room, throwing her hand up to shield her eyes. "This purple is so bright, Rosie. I don't know how you're going to sleep in here."

"You think my room's bad, you should see Carrie's. Did you see that green glow out in the hallway?"

Grandma laughed. "Your mom wants you two to help in the kitchen."

"Aw, Carrie and I wanted to finish unpacking our rooms. Then we were going to hang up our horse posters."

"You'll have beds to sleep in, that's all you two need right now," Grandma said. "You would like to eat tonight wouldn't you?"

"I guess so," Rosie agreed. "I don't know how we're going to get all this done before Thanksgiving."

"We'll make it," Eric said. "The hard part is over."

115

Early the next week the family had everything unpacked and arranged in the new house. Preparations for the Thanksgiving meal began on Wednesday.

Rosie and Carrie stood at the sink peeling potatoes. "How many people are coming tomorrow?" Rosie tossed the potato she had just finished into a bowl. "This seems like enough to feed an army."

"Keep peeling," Grandma directed. "There will be twelve of us, counting Billy and his father."

Rosie frowned. "Why do they have to come?"

Grandma threw the dish towel on the counter and gave Rosie a stern look. "They are coming because your father invited them, and you, young lady, will make Billy feel welcome or you can spend the day in your room!"

Rosie stared at the potato in her hand. Her eyes burned. She fought back tears. Her grandmother had never been this angry with her before. "I'm sorry," she said softly.

Carrie grabbed another potato and peeled it rapidly, removing huge chunks of potato along with the peel.

"God didn't call us to love only the people who are easy to love. He told us to love our enemies. You need to give Billy another chance." Grandma gave Rosie a hug. "I'm sorry I snapped at you."

A big tear rolled down Rosie's cheek. She wiped it off on her sleeve. "It's okay."

"I didn't become a Christian until I was a lot older than Billy. You wouldn't have liked me when I was younger either."

Rosie looked up at her grandmother. "You couldn't have been as bad as Billy."

Grandma nodded slowly. "Probably worse. When you don't have God in your life, you tend to do stupid things. God surrounded me with people who never gave up on me, and finally I realized He was the only solution to the mess I had made of my life."

Rosie turned the potato over in her hands. It was hard for her to believe her grandmother had ever been anything like Billy. She glanced over at her. Grandma had a look that said she didn't want to talk about it anymore, so Rosie quietly resumed peeling.

Rosie crawled into bed that night and stared at the ceiling. Could she forgive Billy? If her grandmother had been that angry with her, maybe her attitude toward him was wrong. Grandma had said there were people in her life who hadn't given up on her; maybe God had sent Billy to her family so they wouldn't give up on him.

*God, help me to give Billy another chance. I'm sorry for how mean I've been to him.*

She fell into a deep, peaceful sleep and woke to the delightful aroma of roast turkey drifting up the stairs. She threw on her clothes and ran downstairs to find Carrie already helping Kristy and Grandma in the kitchen.

"Hey, no fair. You never get up before me," Rosie said.

"I was excited about Thanksgiving. It's my first holiday with my new family."

Kristy leaned over and gave Carrie a hug.

Grandma opened the oven door. A fresh wave of delicious odors—roast turkey, with sage stuffing—drifted across the kitchen. "We're finished with everything we can do for now. We just have to wait for the turkey to finish cooking."

Rosie's mouth watered. She could feel her stomach rumbling. "I can't wait until we eat. Everything smells so good." Since she had slept through breakfast, she grabbed a freshly baked roll off the counter to tide her over until the meal was ready.

"I've already taken care of the horses," Eric told the girls.

"Thanks, Dad." The weight of the grudge Rosie had carried against Billy had lifted sometime during the night, and she felt happier than she had in a long time. "Come on, Carrie, let's bring in some firewood."

The girls slipped on their coats and went to the front door. Rosie stopped and looked out the window, motioning to Carrie. "Look."

Tick and Cowboy were curled up, sleeping side-by-side on the porch. "Aren't they cute together?"

The gangly teenage Rottweiler had adopted the kitten Rosie had brought home from the woods and now the two were practically inseparable.

Carrie laughed. "We have such strange animals—a cat that likes to ride horses and now seems to think he is a dog."

Rosie opened the door and scooped up the kitten. She held him in her arms like a baby and scratched his soft belly. He lay contentedly purring and blinking his eyes. "Do you want to go for another ride, little Cowboy?"

She set the kitten down and ran toward the shed where the firewood was stored. Carrie, Tick, and the kitten tagged along behind her. Rosie opened the shed door and held both arms straight out in front of her. "Stack me up."

Cowboy scrambled up to the top of the pile, scratching his claws on the wood, while Carrie placed one log after another on her sister's arms. When the stack reached Rosie's chin she called out, "That's enough!" and started for the house. Tick snatched one of the smaller logs and trotted after her.

Carrie hurriedly grabbed a few logs and ran to catch up. Rosie had so much wood stacked in front of her she had to walk sideways to see where she was going.

Tick brought her contribution into the house behind the girls. Eric took the slobbery piece of wood from the dog's mouth. "Why, thank you, Tick. Are those mean girls making you do all the work? You poor thing." He patted her head. The dog looked up at him and seemed to smile.

Rosie and Carrie returned for another load while Tick went to explore the interesting smells coming from the kitchen. When the girls were finished, they hung their coats in the back room and returned to the living room.

Carrie stood looking out the window. "Someone's coming down the drive!"

"Is it Aunt Julie?" Rosie nudged Carrie over so she could see.

Kristy looked into the living room from the kitchen. "Stop spying on our guests."

"It must be Billy's dad's car," Carrie said. The girls stepped back from the window and waited impatiently, but no one came to the door.

"What are they doing out there?" Rosie asked. "It doesn't take that long to walk to the front porch." She started toward the window again, but her dad pulled her back.

Finally the doorbell rang, and the girls raced to answer it. Billy stood awkwardly on the porch with his father beside him.

"Come in," Carrie said.

"I'm glad you could come," Rosie mumbled. She held out her hand toward Billy. "May I take your coat?"

Billy stared at her. He slowly removed his coat and handed it over.

"Thanks for coming." Eric held out his hand to Billy's father. "You can't imagine how thankful we are for Billy. If it weren't for him we wouldn't be having this meal here today."

Mr. King shook Eric's hand and smiled. He seemed surprised, as if he had rarely heard anyone compliment his son.

"Oh, this is my dad, Daniel." Billy gestured toward his father. "Dad, this is Eric—er Mr. Jackson."

Rosie pointed out the window. "Aunt Julie's coming!"

Carrie opened the door, then looked down. "No, June Bug. Stay out!" She started to shut the door, but the bobtailed calico slipped past her into the house. "Rosie, grab her! She has something in her mouth."

Rosie shook her head. No one ever tried to pick up June Bug except Grandma. The cat darted across the living room and into the kitchen with Rosie and Carrie close behind. Tick joined in the excitement, barking and running around the room.

June Bug stopped under the kitchen table, dropped the mouse she had been carrying and looked up at Grandma as if to say, "I brought you something!"

The little mouse stood frozen with fear for a moment, then made a beeline straight for Kristy, who screamed and jumped onto a chair. "Eric! You said she would keep the mice away. Now she's bringing them right into the house!"

Rosie rolled her eyes and laughed. "It's only a mouse, Mom."

When June Bug realized the mouse had escaped, she took off after it. Tick hadn't even noticed the mouse, but she thought chasing the cat was great fun. Billy jumped out of her way to keep from being knocked over by the enthusiastic Rottweiler.

"Someone catch June Bug," Carrie yelled. "She's going to kill it!"

Rosie saw Grandma hurrying back into the kitchen with a broom. She wasn't sure whether her grandmother planned to use it on the mouse or the cat. The answer was both. First she tried to sweep the mouse into a corner, but it scurried around the edge of the broom, and June Bug pounced on it. Grandma swatted the cat with the broom and sent her flying into the living room with Tick racing after her. She finally corralled the mouse in a corner of the kitchen where it cowered behind the broom, whiskers quivering.

"Pick it up, Grandma," Carrie said.

Grandma shook her head. "I'm not touching it."

Billy stepped past the girls, knelt down, and grabbed the mouse by its tail. He dangled the petrified creature upside down. "It's just a little field mouse."

"Eww," Kristy shuddered. "Get that thing out of here!"

At that moment Julie stepped into the kitchen. Her eyes widened when she saw Kristy standing on the chair, then she turned to Billy and shook her head. "Uh, if that's what you all are serving for Thanksgiving, I'm going back home!"

The mouse escapade hadn't dampened Rosie's appetite. The smells from the kitchen tormented her. She didn't think she'd ever been so hungry. Finally the turkey was fully cooked, and everyone gathered around the large table in the dining room. There was so much food the table sagged in the middle. They all joined hands as Eric asked the blessing over the meal.

Kristy started a plate heaped with turkey around the table. "I thought it would be nice if we each said something we were thankful for this year."

Rosie smiled. "Like June Bug?"

"Now, don't be mean to your mother on Thanksgiving," Grandma laughed.

"Right," Eric said. "Or we'll have to start telling possum stories."

Rosie shook her head vigorously. "No, please don't." If Billy heard the possum story, she knew he would never stop teasing her about it.

"I'll start," Kristy said. "I can think of two big things this year. First, of course, I'm thankful for our new daughter, Carrie." She smiled at Carrie who was seated across from her. "A close second is that Mom wasn't hurt any worse in the accident."

"I say what Mom said and that we got this farm," Rosie said in between mouthfuls of mashed potatoes. "Oh! And I'm thankful for Cowboy, our new kitty."

"I'm thankful for Billy's help with the house," Eric said. "Your son's a great worker, Daniel."

Billy's face turned a little red. He stared at his plate.

"I'm thankful for his help with Sassy. That mule's a different animal since Billy's been riding her," Julie added.

When Grandma's turn came, she looked thoughtful for a moment. "I have so many things I'm thankful for."

"Could you keep it down to a dozen or so, Mom?" Julie laughed.

"If you insist. I'm thankful to have the cast off my leg and to be able to ride again. And thankful that Kezzie is recovering so well. There's also that new granddaughter I have." She winked at Carrie. "And that I can live here with my daughter and son-in-law!"

Grandma nodded to Carrie.

"I'm thankful for my new family, that I became a Christian, and for my new horse." Carrie hurried through her list.

When they reached the end of the table, Eric said, "Would you like to say anything, Billy?"

Billy hesitated. "I'm thankful that you asked me to work here." He turned and smiled at Grandma and Julie. "And that you let me ride Sassy."

"I guess that leaves me," Daniel said. "Thank you for inviting us today. I can't remember when I've had a meal this delicious. And thank you for having Billy work for you. It hasn't been easy raising him by myself, and—well, he's run a bit wild at times."

Billy looked sideways at his dad as if he wanted him to stop talking, but his father continued. "He's loved working here. He would come home at night and tell me everything that happened each day." Daniel looked around the table. "I feel like I already know all of you."

Eric cleared his throat. "Could you spare him next spring? Or do you need him at your place, Daniel?"

Billy sat up straighter. He gave Eric a quick look, then turned to his father.

"I don't have much for him to do at our place, what with the horses all gone now," Daniel said.

"I guess I should ask you if you want to keep working here, Billy," Eric said.

"Sure." A big smile spread across his face.

"I can't afford to pay you much right away, but if the summer camps do well, I could pay you more later. You can stay in the apartment in the barn, and you're welcome to eat your meals with us."

"Sounds good to me," Billy said. "What do you need?"

"You any good with a chainsaw?" Jonathan asked. "We need to clear the trails."

"I was born with a chainsaw in my hands," Billy laughed.

Rosie shook her head. *Oh, no, here we go again.* Seeing how pleased Billy was about being able to continue working at Sonrise Stable made her feel good inside. There might be some advantages to having someone like a big brother around the place.

"We need to build the bunkhouses in the barn," Eric added.

"And split more firewood," Jonathan said.

"Don't forget mule training," Julie added.

Billy looked back and forth as more and more work was added. His smile was growing.

"Sounds like you're going to be busy, Billy," Grandma said.

After everyone had eaten a little too much they moved to the living room, talking and letting their food settle. It wasn't long before Rosie grew tired of sitting around. "I'm going to go ride. Anyone want to join me?"

"I bet Scamper will be thankful for that," Jared laughed. "What a great holiday for him."

"Ha," Rosie said. "He's thankful that I'm his owner."

"I'm going to have another piece of pumpkin pie." Jared patted his stomach and headed for the kitchen.

"I'll ride," Carrie said.

"Me too," said Jamie. Jessie nodded.

Rosie glanced awkwardly at Billy. "Would you like to ride with us?"

Billy jumped to his feet. "Uh, no. We need to be going. Don't we, Dad?"

Rosie and Carrie ran to get their coats for them.

Daniel waved to everyone as Billy pushed him toward the door. "Thanks again for the meal—for everything."

Rosie watched Billy hurry to the car. *What's wrong with him? I try to be nice to him, and that's how he acts? Oh, well.* She shook her head and turned to the other girls. "Race you to the barn!"

The others were hard on her heels, but Rosie reached the barn first. She pushed the sliding door open and stepped inside. As her eyes adjusted to the dimmer light, she noticed something on the front of Scamper's stall. "That's odd." She stopped and stared for a moment, waiting for Carrie to catch up.

"What's that?" Carrie asked breathlessly.

"I don't know." Rosie moved closer, and her mouth dropped open. "A trophy—and a blue ribbon?" She carefully untied the trophy, held it up, and read the engraving out loud. "Western Pony Pleasure – Union County Fair." She turned the ribbon over. Scrawled on the back, in handwriting she could barely read, was a single word—*Sorry.*

She looked at Carrie. They both smiled and said, "Billy."

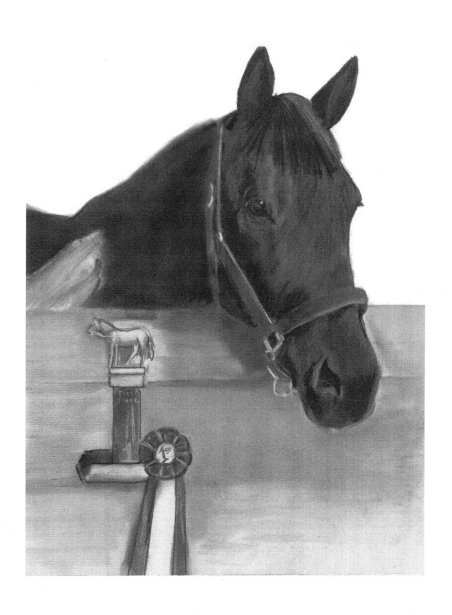

# The Sonrise Stable Series
# Book 4: Tender Mercies

When Rosie, Carrie, and Grandma are asked to help out at Last Chance Corral, a horse and foal rescue, Rosie is shocked when she experiences firsthand how cruel some people can be to animals. During the week at Last Chance, the girls learn that the God who knows when a sparrow falls to the ground works through the kindness of others to provide for the animals He created. For the foals, and the girls, Last Chance Corral is a life-changing experience.

**Book 1: Rosie and Scamper**

**Book 2: Carrie and Bandit**

**Book 3: Clothed with Thunder**

Available at www.sonrisestable.com

# Amazingly Designed—From Head to Hoof

Here is a sampling of the anatomical features that point to the horse having an Intelligent Designer.

## Hoof

The hoof is a complicated structure consisting of sole, frog, hoof wall, lamina, coffin bone, digital cushion, navicular bone, and short pastern bone. These parts work together to support the horse's weight and provide traction, shock absorption and proper blood flow through the legs.

## Pastern

The slope of the horse's shoulder, pastern, and hoof should all match. The horse's pastern serves an important role in absorbing shock as the horse moves.

## Cannon

Although it averages a mere nine inches in circumference, the cannon bone is crucial to the horse's anatomy since it is the primary weight-bearing bone in the leg. The cannon bone runs from the knee to the fetlock.

## Eyes

Horses' eyes are located on the sides of their heads, giving them a much larger field of vision than humans, about 350 degrees. Horses have small blind spots directly in front and behind; however a slight shift of the head brings those areas into view. They can see color, but not as well as humans. Their distance and night vision are better than that of humans.

## Ears

In addition to hearing, horses use their ears to communicate with humans and other horses. Ears flattened against the horse's head indicate annoyance or anger. The funnel shape of the horse's ear captures and conducts sound to the inner ear. Horses can rotate their ears to hear sounds coming from different directions. Each ear can move independently up to 180 degrees. Ten different muscles control ear movement. Hairs inside the ear help keep dirt and insects out. Horses can hear higher pitched sounds than humans, but not as high as those a dog or cat can hear.

## Teeth

Horses have twelve incisors at the front of the mouth for grazing. Behind the front incisors is the interdental space, which contains no teeth. In the back of their mouths are twelve premolars and twelve molars used for chewing and grinding food. Some horses also have varying numbers of canine or wolf teeth.

Horses' teeth never stop growing. They wear against the tooth above or below them. The age of a horse can be roughly determined by the number, size, shape, and angle of its teeth.

## Tail

The tail is an extension of the horse's spinal column and serves as a very accurate fly swatter. It is also used for communication. Movement and position of the tail can indicate annoyance, fright, discomfort, and more.

## Respiratory System

A horse cannot breathe through its mouth, only through its nostrils, because the nasal passages are separated from the oral cavity. The nostrils expand greatly during exercise to take in more air. Horses cannot pant.

Horses have something called *guttural pouches*, large air pockets on each side of the back of the throat. The exact purpose of the pouches is unclear. One idea is that they cool blood traveling to the brain when a horse is exercising.

At rest, a horse normally breathes eight to twelve times per minute. Horses can take in twice as much oxygen as humans for an equivalent body weight.

At a canter or gallop, a horse's breathing is timed with its stride. The horse inhales when its front hooves are striding outward and exhales when all four legs come together. In a typical race a horse will move the equivalent of two five-gallon buckets of air into and out of its lungs every second. If all the airways in a horse's lungs were laid out flat on the ground, they would cover ten tennis courts.

## Circulatory System

A horse's heart beats 28 to 45 times per minute at rest, but it can go up to 250 during strenuous exercise. The heart and blood vessels of the average horse contain approximately 9 gallons of blood. The heart of an average horse weighs 8.5 pounds. The heart of the famous racehorse, Secretariat, was estimated to weigh 22 pounds. It is believed that a certain gene, called the X factor, is responsible for the abnormally large hearts found in some horses.

## Digestive System
The horse's digestive tract is a complicated system, approximately 100 feet long. The esophagus (4.5 feet long) carries food to the stomach (8 to 17 quarts). A one-way valve in the esophagus prevents horses from vomiting.

After the food is processed in the stomach, it passes to the small intestine, the major organ of digestion in the horse (70 feet long, 48 quarts). Digested food is absorbed through the walls of the small intestine into the blood stream. Any food not digested in the small intestine passes into the large intestine or hind gut which consists of the cecum (4 feet, 32 quarts), large colon (12 feet, 80 quarts), small colon (12 feet, 14 quarts) and rectum (1 foot).

Horses were designed to eat small amounts of food frequently throughout the day. Modern changes to the horse's diet— moving to larger, less frequent feedings can introduce problems such as colic.

## Sense of Smell
Due to the length of the nasal cavity, the horse has a better sense of smell than humans. The flehmen response, a curling of the upper lip, allows horses to process scents through the Jacobson's organ located on the roof of their mouths.

## Sleep
Unlike humans, horses do not need a solid, unbroken period of sleep. Most of their sleep occurs in short intervals of about fifteen minutes each for a total of about three hours per day. A stay apparatus in their legs allows horses to enter light sleep while standing up. This is achieved by tendons and ligaments

in the legs locking into place, allowing the horse to carry its weight on two front legs and one hind leg, with the other hind resting on its toe.

### Skin
The body of the horse is covered with a layer of panniculus muscles just under the skin. These muscles produce the twitching response used to remove flies that land on the horse. A horse's lower legs and head do not have these muscles, so horses stomp or toss their heads when flies land in those areas.

### Winter and Summer Coats
Horses can grow thick coats for warmth and shed them to smooth sleek coats in warmer seasons. The changes in coat length are not triggered by temperature, but by the number of daylight hours.

### Velvety Muzzles
Is there anything softer than a horse's muzzle? There is nothing about a velvety-soft muzzle that would give the horse any evolutionary advantage, but God knew how soothing it would be for those who love horses to stroke that soft skin!

### Additional Resources
For links to resources on horse anatomy and physiology, check the *Clothed With Thunder* book page at www.sonrisestable.com

# eQuest For Truth

If you'd like to learn more about the origin of the horse from a creationist perspective, a good place to start is the website *eQuest 4 Truth*. Founded in 2006 by Rebekah Holt, *eQuest 4 Truth* provides a wealth of information about creation, evolution, and horses in the Bible.

Rebekah is the third in a family of ten homeschooled children—the oldest daughter. Eight of the children and both parents ride. Rebekah's love for horses was evident from an early age. As a toddler on their Texas farm she stole away to sit on her family's pony, Sugar Plum, who was stretched out, fast asleep in the backyard. At the age of ten, she began saving to buy a horse of her own. Within a year she was able to purchase a beautiful chestnut filly named Acey and later trained the horse with the help of her father.

As an adult, Rebekah became a certified riding instructor and used Acey to teach her younger siblings and other children how to ride. As she and her students worked with the horses, Rebekah began to weave spiritual truths into the conversations.

"Do you know who made the horse?" or "When God created horses, He made the frog to help cushion the foot."

Rebekah's goals for *eQuest 4 Truth* are to uphold biblical Christianity in equestrian education and to refute fallacies that deny God as the Creator and Jesus Christ as our risen Savior.

When she's not teaching, riding, or training horses, she enjoys cooking, sewing, drawing, painting, photography, writing, and playing the piano. If the Lord blesses her with a Christian husband, Rebekah would love to be a stay-at-home homeschool mom, just like her own mother.

In addition to all the great creation information about horses, *eQuest 4 Truth* offers annual art, photography, and writing contests.

Check it all out at www.equest4truth.com

For additional creation resource links, visit the *Clothed With Thunder* book page at www.sonrisestable.com.